"Could we... that night?"

Lorna asked.

"I guess that was an unusual night for both of us." Jess believed anything she told him, he realized. But he still had the nagging sense that there was something else she hadn't told him.

"I'd like to take you to dinner," he said, sounding as casual as possible while he thought about what her body felt like. And how sweet she tasted when she parted her lips for his kiss. He wanted her more than he wanted to breathe.

"It's not necessary," she replied. "Honest."

"I'd like to anyway."

"I can't."

"Are you involved with someone else?" Jess wondered, ignoring a fierce stab of jealousy.

She shook her head.

"Then you're free to have dinner with me Friday night."

"Mr. Sheridan, I *really* can't go out with you."

"Call me Jess," he said. "I'll pick you up at seven." He turned quickly and went down the porch steps. He didn't want to hear her objections, didn't want to hear her refuse his invitation.

He was a patient man. He could wait until Friday.

Dear Reader,

Welcome once again to Beauville, Texas!

Blame It on Babies was such fun to write, especially
when it opened with Jake and Elizabeth's wedding
in the town square. Pookie is there, wearing a tux in
honor of the festivities, and so are all the cowhands
from the Dead Horse Ranch. A waitress serving
barbecued ribs at the reception and a bitterly divorced
wedding guest end up together at the end of the
evening. Six months later, Jess and Lorna's volatile
romance gives the townspeople *lots* to talk about!

You'll meet these characters again, plus some other
familiar friends, in my next book, *Blame it on Texas*,
a Harlequin single title available in March 2001. You'll
see what happened to Elizabeth and Jake, plus learn
a few of the town's best-kept secrets, when the Good
Night Drive In is turned into a retirement home and
Dustin Jones, former cowhand at the Dead Horse
Ranch, meets up with his first love.

I love hearing from readers, so please let me know
what characters you'd like to see again in future
Beauville stories.

Best wishes!

Kristine Rolofson
P.O. Box 323
Peace Dale, RI 02883

Books by Kristine Rolofson

HARLEQUIN TEMPTATION
765—BILLY AND THE KID
802—BLAME IT ON COWBOYS*

* Boots & Beauties

BLAME IT ON BABIES
Kristine Rolofson

ISBN 0-373-25919-0

BLAME IT ON BABIES

Copyright © 2001 by Kristine Rolofson.

All rights reserved. Except for use in any review, the reproduction or
utilization of this work in whole or in part in any form by any electronic,
mechanical or other means, now known or hereafter invented, including
xerography, photocopying and recording, or in any information storage
or retrieval system, is forbidden without the written permission of the
publisher, Harlequin Enterprises Limited, 225 Duncan Mill Road,
Don Mills, Ontario, Canada M3B 3K9.

All characters in this book have no existence outside the imagination of
the author and have no relation whatsoever to anyone bearing the same
name or names. They are not even distantly inspired by any individual
known or unknown to the author, and all incidents are pure invention.

This edition published by arrangement with Harlequin Books S.A.

® and TM are trademarks of the publisher. Trademarks indicated with
® are registered in the United States Patent and Trademark Office, the
Canadian Trade Marks Office and in other countries.

Visit us at www.eHarlequin.com

Printed in U.S.A.

HARLEQUIN®

TORONTO • NEW YORK • LONDON
AMSTERDAM • PARIS • SYDNEY • HAMBURG
STOCKHOLM • ATHENS • TOKYO • MILAN • MADRID
PRAGUE • WARSAW • BUDAPEST • AUCKLAND

ISBN 0-373-25919-0

BLAME IT ON BABIES

Copyright © 2001 by Kristine Rolofson.

Printed in U.S.A.

1

JESS SHERIDAN HAD NO USE for weddings. He was only attending this one out of respect for the man standing next to the bride, an impressively beautiful woman he'd seen shopping in town a few times. She'd looked pleasant enough...but didn't they all?

Until the ring went on their finger, that is.

He watched Jake Johnson kiss his bride and applauded with the rest of the Beauville residents as the justice of the peace pronounced them married. Then he acknowledged Jake's grin as the groom walked Mrs. Johnson back up the makeshift aisle toward the blue-and-white striped tent set up in the corner of the park. There'd be a makeshift bar in that tent, considering the amount of ice he'd seen being unloaded in that direction. No one would go thirsty this afternoon, not if the rumors were true about Jake sparing no expense to celebrate his sudden wedding to someone he'd known only a few weeks. The man was taking a chance, Jess figured, but no one had asked his opinion so he kept it to himself.

A cold beer would go down real good right now,

considering a July afternoon in Texas had to be what hell felt like. Lucky he was used to it, like most folks around here, or else they'd expire before the barbecue ribs and corn bread were served over in the Grange Hall across the street. Jess looked around and saw some of the hands from the Dead Horse looking as if they were as thirsty as he was. Young Calhoun looked pale, probably hungover, if the rumors were right about him being dumped before getting married himself and drowning his sorrows in Jack Daniels ever since.

The kid spotted him, which made Jess wish he'd hurried to the beer tent a little faster.

"Sheridan!"

"Calhoun." Jess braced himself for an onslaught of questions, but the group of men from the Dead Horse seemed uncharacteristically silent. "Nice wedding," was all he could think of to say. Inwardly he wondered if Jake would be able to keep his ranch after the divorce or would his wife carry a bag of money back to wherever it was in New England she came from.

"What a shindig!" The young man wiped his brow with the back of his sleeve. "I'm glad that's over. Jake made us wear these neckties."

"And iron our shirts," Old Shorty griped. "But Miz Elizabeth sure looked pretty, didn't she?"

"Yeah. Most brides do."

Dusty Jones, the cowhand closer to his own age

than the others, gave him a sharp look. And then he smiled, as if he knew darn well what other things Jess had been thinking.

"She's a nice lady. And they'll do just fine," the man declared. "Jake's a happy man today."

Bobby sighed. "I should've been a married man last week. Amy Lou and I were gonna get married on the Fourth of July."

Shorty rolled his eyes. "Yeah, well, your heart's been broken a few hundred times before this one, so you'll get over it."

"I saw the Wynette twins heading toward the beer tent," Dusty said. "You might drown your sorrows in that direction."

Calhoun brightened, his broken heart obviously forgotten with the news that the blond barrel racers were starting to drink. Billy Martin, his ever-present cohort, looked more cheerful, too. "Well, I guess we'd all better get us a cold beer."

Shorty shook his head. "We're supposed to go into the line," he told them. "Shake Jake's hand and kiss the bride and all that."

"The receiving line," Jess felt compelled to point out, "starts over there by the bar."

He would have laughed at the expression of relief on the men's faces, but he didn't think anything was funny today. In a few short hours he was leaving

Beauville, and he didn't care if he never returned. "Where's Roy?"

"He elected to stay at the ranch," Bobby said. "He's not much for crowds."

"I'd better go get that dog," Shorty said. "I promised Miz Elizabeth I'd keep him out of the sun."

"And away from the ladies," Bobby added. "The little critter likes to pee on just about anything."

"Better keep Billy away from the ladies too, with his luck," Shorty joked, earning an elbow in the ribs from Marty.

"He's right. I have the worst damn luck with women," the young cowboy grumbled, but his gaze was on the beer tent. The receiving line was moving right along.

"I think I win that prize," Jess said, tipping his hat lower on his forehead. The four men stared at him, then looked at the ground, the beer tent, the sky and the two matronly ladies who walked past them.

"Well," Shorty drawled, after swallowing hard, "not every man gets as lucky as Jake."

"I'll drink to that," Bobby offered, and broke into his usual grin. Jess had to hand it to him. The boy was sure good-natured, like his father and grandfather, if the stories were right.

"And so will I," Jess agreed, starting toward the line of people waiting to congratulate the newly married couple. A beer was sounding better by the minute in this heat. He wasn't going to stay for the food or the dancing; he wasn't going to give the town biddies a chance to look at him and gossip about his marriage and all the things that Susan had done behind his back.

Jess and the boys from the Dead Horse got in line behind a tall brunette with legs up to her chin and a plump redhead with a chest that could make a man weep for mercy. After the obligatory congratulations to the bride and groom, Jess stepped aside and left the flirting to Calhoun and Marty, two young men who had yet to discover that women were trouble and should be avoided at all costs.

THE BRIDE WORE GREEN. A cool, minty silver shade of the palest green that showed off her golden tan and chestnut hair. Lorna Walters would bet a million dollars the woman's eyes were a similar mossy shade. It would be stunning, she thought, wishing she was closer to see what was going on, but she'd signed on to serve barbecue ribs and she didn't think the bride would be beckoning her over any time soon.

The bride was carrying a dog. Or at least, Lorna thought it was a dog. It was hairy and wore a tuxedo, so it could have been a monkey. But she'd heard Martha McIntosh, the town clerk, whisper to a younger redheaded woman that the bride thought her little dog should be at the wedding, at least for a while. A dog in a tuxedo would certainly keep the townspeople talking for a while. That and the green bridal gown that didn't look like a bridal gown. The new Mrs. Jake Johnson must be an original thinker.

Beauville wasn't used to original thinkers, Lorna didn't suppose.

Lorna basted ribs with Texas Tom's Secret Barbecue Sauce and thought about weddings and men and one man in particular. He was here. She'd spotted him standing off to one side, staring at the bride and groom as if he'd never seen anything more horrifying than a man and a woman getting married.

She guessed she couldn't blame him. Everyone in town had known what Sue was doing behind her husband's back—except her husband. Even Lorna had heard about it and she'd been living in Dallas at the time.

That's when she'd been employed, with a roof over her head and enough money to pay for gasoline and food and a closet full of clothes and shoes. She still had the car, the clothes and an impressive collection of shoes, but the job? Basting ribs and wearing a spattered canvas apron over her waitress uniform certainly proved what her mother had always warned, "Pride goeth before a fall, Lorna, so you'd better not get too big for your britches."

Well, her britches would be spattered with barbecue sauce too if she wasn't careful.

"Lorna!" Texas Tom waved his spatula at her. "Quit daydreaming and turn that batch over."

"Okay," she hollered back, and obligingly picked up the tongs. What was a little smoke? The crunchy edges only made the ribs taste better, Lorna knew, but she did as she was told before glancing toward the crowd across the grass at the beer tent. They'd be looking for platters of ribs soon, and Lorna hoped she'd be the one carrying the food next door to the Grange. Texas Tom had set up his barbecue grills in the park, as close to the Grange as he could get without interfering with the crowd of wedding guests. The smoke puffed away from the people and the ovens were placed so that inquisitive onlookers could look at the sizzling beef but not get close enough to burn themselves.

Jess Sheridan was somewhere in the crowd. If she could see through the smoke she might spot him. If she was lucky he might even take a rib or two from her tray. He would say, "I could never resist a woman who smells like smoked hickory," and then he would sweep her into his arms and—

"Get those ribs in back out of the flames, dammit!" Texas Tom didn't have a lot of patience for novices, not when his reputation was at stake. He did glance

once again at Lorna's breasts, as if he was trying to
see them through the thick fabric of the apron.

"No problem," Lorna said, trying not to burn herself despite the thick oven mitts she'd found in a box
of spices and paper towels.

"Never mind," the fat little cook sputtered. Texas
Tom wasn't known for his wonderful personality. He
took the tongs out of her hand and pointed to the platters piled with smoking pork. "Take those into the
Grange and put them on the long tables set up across
from the desserts. And try not to drop anything."

"I won't," she promised, catching the wink of the
other worker, a teenaged boy who was in the unfor-
tunate situation of having the "Texas BBQ King" for
an uncle. She smiled at him and, dropping her gloves
on the makeshift table, wiped her perspiring face
with a clean paper towel. There were advantages to
seeing Jess Sheridan at a distance, especially since she
had never looked worse. Not that he would recognize
her anyway.

"And get that hair out of your face," came another
order from the old ogre. Lorna complied, managing
to redo her curly ponytail in one practiced motion.

Lorna picked up one of the heavy platters and got a
good grip on the handles before heading to the
Grange. She also had to get a grip on her imagination.
She had as much of a chance with Jess Sheridan as
Texas Tom did with her: Absolutely zero.

HE NOTICED HER. And he was certain other men did, too, though Jess didn't see any of them bothering her while she refilled the rib platters and replaced empty pots of barbecued beans with full ones. She worked hard, managing to carry salads and platters and all sorts of food back and forth between the catering trucks and the Grange.

This particular woman would be difficult to ignore. Tiny, curves in all the right places, from what he could tell. She moved like a woman who was aware of exactly what she was doing to every man there at the Johnson wedding. Golden, almost silver, curls tumbled around her face and down her neck, as the ponytail at the back of her head loosened. Blue eyes, he'd guess, though he hadn't been close enough to see for himself. Her face was flushed, though the color looked good on her.

He shouldn't watch her, and he didn't. Not too much, anyway. He didn't think he'd ever seen her before, so she must have come with the Texas Tom employees. No way was she related to the BBQ King, not with that complexion and that hair. He hoped she got paid well, hoped she'd find another job that didn't require carrying other people's garbage.

But mostly he just wished she'd go away. He didn't particularly like that he was watching her like some pervert.

"Mr. Sheridan?" He looked to his right to see the

bride looking up at him, her expression a little uncertain. He wondered if he'd been frowning, so he forced himself to look pleasant.

"Mrs. Johnson?"

"Please, call me Elizabeth."

"If you call me Jess. My first name is really Jester, but only my mother ever got away with calling me that."

"Thank you." The bride's smile widened, which was what Jess intended. He knew he was overly tall and overly large, but that came in handy in his profession. Smiling didn't.

"What can I do for you, Elizabeth?"

"Jake and I wanted to thank you for coming today. We're getting ready to leave for our honeymoon, but I realized there were still people I hadn't had a chance to talk to."

"Thanks for inviting me. I wouldn't have missed it," Jess lied, knowing damn well he would have used any excuse he could think up to avoid watching a wedding take place. "Jake's a good friend." That was the truth. Jess looked past the bride to see the groom heading their way. He looked like a man who was ready for his wedding night, especially when his arm went around his bride and he reached out to shake Jess's hand. Jess didn't think he'd ever seen his friend so happy. Lord, he hoped it would last. At least for a couple of years.

"Thanks for coming."

Jess cleared his throat. "Yeah. Where're you headed now?"

"To the airport," Elizabeth said. "We leave for Boston tomorrow morning."

"We're spending a couple of weeks in New England. I always wanted to see the ocean."

"The boys at the Dead Horse can survive without you?"

Jake shook his head. "Probably not, but we're moving out to my place. Permanently. Bobby's going to have to find another foreman."

"Or do the work himself," Jess added.

"Exactly." The men shared a smile. The thought of that wild-ass cowboy actually running his own place seemed ludicrous. "I guess it has to happen sooner or later."

"Bobby will do just fine," the bride declared. "And so will the ranch."

"Yes, ma'am," Jess said to Elizabeth, but his mind was on the yellow-haired waitress whom he could see out of the corner of his eye clearing the table near where they stood. That damn apron mostly hid her body, but he'd bet his last paycheck it was the kind of body a man would remember.

"Shorty's moving out to my place to take care of things while we're gone," Jake said, and Jess struggled to turn his attention back to his friend. He'd thought for a moment he recognized the woman, but on second look he doubted it. He would have remembered.

"Sounds good," he agreed, shaking Jake's hand once again as the couple bid him goodbye. He turned his attention once again to the blond gal, but she was busy handing out wedding cake and he couldn't see her face. So he decided to have another drink. It would be whiskey instead of beer. He would join the crowd gathered outside and drink to Jake's good fortune.

As the day wore on and drew closer to sundown, Jess freely sampled the whiskey and paid vague attention to the festivities. "Yeah," he said in response to Calhoun's words, lifting another glass to toast to...something. He hadn't heard what Calhoun announced, but every other man standing at the edge of the tent looked damned impressed. The plump redhead was stuck to Bobby's side like a tick, so the kid obviously wasn't pining too hard for his lost fiancée. "Better watch out, Calhoun," he muttered, lifting his empty glass. Someone filled it up again, which was exactly what he'd hoped would happen.

Teenage twins draped themselves over Billy Martin, Shorty sat in the shade with a flat-faced dog asleep on his lap, and a country-western band wailed from the bandstand in the center of the small park. Jake and his bride had spared no expense to keep the party going, even though they'd left town a while ago. He figured they must have invited everyone in the county to the wedding.

Thank God he didn't have to work tonight. He had the next two days off, and Jess intended to make the most of his last hours in town. He was going to get good and drunk, drunk enough to forget that his wife had emptied their bank account and run off with a man from nearby Marysville. Drunk enough to forget that yesterday the divorce was final. And drunk enough to forget what she'd called him when she left.

Unfortunately, Jess didn't think there was enough booze in Beauville to blot out the memory of his ex-wife.

SHE WOULD NEVER, EVER WORK for Texas Tom again, not if it meant having to load her possessions into a couple of stray grocery carts and live in the parking lot behind the hardware store. When he wasn't leering at her chest, he was shouting orders. She didn't know which one was worse; at least when he was leering she didn't have to listen to the sound of his voice.

"Lorna!" She turned to see the fat toad gesturing toward another pile of garbage. Unfortunately the bags were made of clear plastic, meaning Texas Tom had seen something inside of them he didn't like.

"What?"

"Those damn cowboys threw the silverware out with the paper plates. You're gonna have to go through all this and make sure none of them forks get lost. I came here with four hundred forks and I'm damn well gonna *leave* with four hundred forks."

She would give four hundred dollars—which would pretty much empty her bank account—to go back to Aunt Carol's little house and soak in a bathtub filled with vanilla-scented water. Going through garbage was not her idea of a great way to end the day. "Look, Tom, don't you think I should finish rinsing dishes?" She was standing there in wet tennis shoes, hose in hand, a stack of platters and various cooking utensils beside her that needed to be cleaned up before Tom's nephew could finish loading everything in the truck.

"Yeah, but 'fore we leave we're counting forks, or someone's gonna pay," he grumbled, his gaze dropping to her bare legs. He'd told her to wear a waitress uniform, so she'd gone to Marysville and spent thirty-seven dollars she could have used for the phone bill. She'd been so happy to find work she hadn't questioned the expense.

"It takes money to make money," her mother always said. And what would it take to paw through mounds of garbage? Rubber gloves and a decent vocabulary of cuss words, Lorna decided. She would curse quietly under her breath so no one would hear her. After all, some of those words might give Texas Tom ideas.

She tried to hurry through the cleaning of the cookware. The sun had set, though lanterns were placed around the tent and over the cleanup area next to the grills. Tom's nephew was a decent enough kid, and the sooner she got the racks cleaned up, the sooner he and his uncle could head back to Marysville. With or without four hundred forks.

"Hey," the nephew said, as she finished the last of the trays and turned off the hose. "How's it goin'?"

"We can't leave until we count the silverware," she told him. "He thinks some of it ended up in the garbage."

"Cripe." The boy picked up all four racks of glassware as easily as if they were filled with paper cups. "He's on that kick again?"

"I'm afraid so."

"I'll help," he offered, "as soon as I get the truck loaded up. I'm about halfway done."

"Don't worry about it." Lorna picked up a lantern and swung it toward the piles of garbage bags. "With any luck it won't take me long. The forks would sink to the bottom of the bags, right?"

He lowered his voice. "My uncle's a real prick sometimes."

"I just want to get paid," Lorna said, setting the lantern on the bed of a truck. "He promised cash."

"Yeah," the boy said. "I know what you mean. Good luck."

Good luck. Was there any such thing? Maybe, maybe not. "Luck" would be having the man of your dreams finally notice you. "Luck" would be landing a job with health benefits and a three-week vacation. Lorna untied the nearest garbage bag and put on a pair of yellow rubber gloves. "Luck" would be never having to work for Texas Tom again.

2

"YOU'RE NOT DRIVING, ARE YOU?"

Jess shook his head at the bartender. "Walkin'," was his reply. He would walk to his truck and sleep in the cab. Wouldn't be the first time, though those days were years ago. In his misspent youth.

Those were the days. Now, at thirty-seven, he couldn't drink much whiskey—or anything else alcoholic for that matter—without hurting himself. It was hardly worth it, but today's wedding preceded by yesterday's divorce were events worth trying to forget.

He set down his last empty glass and, stepping over the bodies of a couple of cowboys who couldn't hold their liquor, managed to exit the tent without embarrassing himself by falling flat on his face. Most everyone had gone home—or on to the bars to finish what they'd started. Even the musicians were packing up, and over in the far corner of the park, lights highlighted the removal of Texas Tom's traveling barbecue feast.

Jess thought he'd parked somewhere over there,

but he wasn't sure. He remembered passing the Grange on his way in, so he figured he was heading in the right direction if he walked toward the lights. As he got closer, he was surprised to see that pretty little waitress rifling through the garbage like a starving dog.

"Honey," he drawled, keeping his voice low so he wouldn't scare her. She jumped anyway, then turned around and stared at him.

"What?"

"Honey," he tried again, reaching for the wallet in his back pocket. "You sure as hell shouldn't be in this pre-pre-predicament." He pulled a couple of twenties out of his wallet and handed them to her.

"What are you doing?" She didn't look too happy to take the money. In fact, she tried to stuff it back into his palm. And succeeded, too, before she took a step backward.

"Buy yourself a decent meal," he said, holding out the bills again. "Decent *meals*," he said, correcting himself. With forty dollars she ought to be able to eat for three days, if she was careful. "No reason to go through garbage for something to eat. Doesn't that cheap bas—Texas Tom give you supper?"

He thought she was going to laugh, but he couldn't see her face too well now that she'd stepped away from the lantern. He'd caught a glimpse of big blue eyes and a set of lips that were made for—well, just about anything a man could think of, he figured.

"I'm looking for forks," she said. "And I'm not hungry, thank you."

"Forks," he repeated, hoping he sounded sober. He'd gotten a little dizzy a second ago when she'd smiled. "What for?"

"Texas Tom is counting the silverware." She retied the garbage bag and set it off to one side with two others. "I have to see if any of his precious forks got thrown out before I can go home."

"Or he'll dock your pay?"

"Probably." She reached for another bag and then shook her head. "I'm done. I found two of them." She pulled them out of her apron pocket to show him. "I guess I've done my duty."

"Maybe some more will turn up in the grass tomorrow," he said, hoping to be helpful. He wasn't so drunk that he couldn't be helpful, after all. And the woman was so damn pretty.

"Yes." She gazed up at him, real friendly and nice. Almost as if she knew him, but Jess didn't think so. A man would remember her, that he was certain of. "You're Jess Sheridan, aren't you?"

"Yes, ma'am." So she did know him, or at least knew who he was. Most folks in town did. He went to take off his Stetson, but realized he was bareheaded. Damn. That hat had cost him a bundle six months ago. And it was probably stomped flat in the beer tent now.

"You've had a lot to drink," she said. "Where are you going?"

"To sleep it off, ma'am. In my truck." He pointed to where he hoped his truck was parked. "Somewhere over there."

"Can you *find* your truck?"

He didn't want to lie to the woman, but then again, a man had his pride. "Yep. No problem."

"Lorna! You wanna stop flirtin' with drunks and start countin' my damn forks like I'm paying you to do?" A short bald guy, built like an Angus bull, came roaring up to the waitress and stopped just short of crashing into her. Jess wasn't so far gone that he didn't see the man's gaze drop to the little lady's chest.

"Who you calling a drunk?" Jess straightened to his full height, which he knew was damn impressive, even in Texas, and glared at the screaming lecher.

"Never mind," the waitress said, and she handed the man the forks. "Here. That's all I found, Tom. And now I'm going home."

"Not so fast, missy," the man said, shaking the forks at her. "We're not done here."

The woman put her hands on her hips. "I've been either basting, chopping, grilling, serving, carrying, cleaning, washing or going through garbage since nine this morning. The place is cleaned up, the day is over and I want my money and I want to go home and go to bed. *Now.*"

Jess stared at her. He'd missed a few of the words, but he got the general idea. The little lady was tired.

"Bed?" Texas Tom grinned at her, but it wasn't a real nice expression. "I'll tuck you in, Lorna, if that's what you want."

"I want today's pay. Eight dollars an hour, plus tips." She wasn't about to back down, something that didn't surprise Jess. When a woman put her hands on her hips like that and started talking, it meant a man better listen. Or run for his life.

Tom glanced at Jess and took his life in his hands. "Get lost, cowboy. Lorna and me have business to take care of."

"Nope. I'm staying right here." Jess wished he hadn't had that last glass of Jack Daniels. "I think you'd better give the lady what she wants."

"You do, huh?" Tom reached into his shirt pocket and pulled out a thick wad of bills. He counted out several and handed them to the waitress. "Hundred bucks plus fifty for the tip. Happy now?"

"Yes." The money disappeared into her apron pocket and her shoulders sagged with relief. "Good night," she said to Jess, and took a step backward.

"'Night," Jess answered, realizing he couldn't put off the search for his truck any longer. Besides, he was starting to get hungry. If he couldn't find his truck maybe he could find the café and get some sustenance. He'd moved out of the circle of light when he heard Texas Tom's voice again.

"Not so fast, babe," the BBQ King said, stepping closer. He lowered his voice, but Jess had hearing like a fox. "There's more where that came from, if you know what I mean. A woman like you could play her cards right and wake up with some money on her pillow."

"Oh, for heaven's sake," the lady sputtered, then Jess heard a gasp. "Stop that!"

He was on Texas Tom in two seconds flat, plucked him by the back of his collar and held him away from the waitress, who looked like she wouldn't mind a piece of him herself.

"The lady said no," Jess drawled. "So I think it's time for you to get into the truck and get out of here, Tom."

Tom kept talking, and nothing was flattering to either Jess or the waitress, so Jess finally got tired of the noise and flung the man into the garbage bags, where he lay gasping for breath and more than a little stunned.

"Thanks." The waitress smiled at him again, and Jess wobbled a little on his size thirteen feet.

"No problem, ma'am." He wished he hadn't lost his hat. He would have held it in his hands and begged her to keep smiling at him. "You need an escort home?"

"I'll be fine," she assured him, after looking over at Tom, who was struggling to get on his feet. "He'll leave me alone now and I have the money he owed me."

"I could walk you home," Jess offered, hoping she lived somewhere in the direction of his truck. Or that he would see the truck on the way.

"Thank you, but—"

Jess barely knew what hit him. But in the moment before he blacked out he realized Texas Tom was the revengeful type.

LORNA SAT in the grass beside the man of her dreams and thought a little bit more about luck. Was this good luck or bad luck? She'd had a crush on Jess Sheridan since she was thirteen and now, years later, she was spending the evening with him. Just because he was snoring and unconscious didn't discount the fact that they were together at last.

Here she'd always hoped he'd notice her, and when he did he thought she was digging for food from the garbage. It wasn't what she'd call good luck, but she'd enjoyed talking to him, even if he'd had too much to drink and acted a little silly and wouldn't remember her in the morning.

She liked looking at him. Lorna peered into his

face, which had always been handsome. His dark hair was a little too short, but it waved nicely on his forehead. He had a large nose that fit his face, and lips that were neither too thin or too plump. His skin was tanned, as if he spent a lot of time outside, and she loved his chin. There was a faint dimple there; she could see its shadow from the corner streetlight and she'd touched it with her index finger just to make sure. His skin was smooth underneath her fingertip; he must have shaved right before the wedding.

He didn't look as if he was in pain. Or dead. He looked peaceful, like he was taking a nap. His breathing was even and sometimes noisy. There'd been no blood. She'd thought about going for help, but that would mean leaving her rescuer alone near the pile of garbage. Which didn't seem at all like the right thing to do.

Texas Tom had left in a hurry, especially after she threatened to call the police. Lorna thought it was her screaming that made Tom run to his truck, with the oversize metal tongs he'd used to hit Jess in the back of the head still in his hand. She'd screamed loud enough to wake the dead, but oddly nobody in Beauville came to her rescue. It was Saturday night and she could hear the music blasting from one of the bars around the corner. The beer tent was still standing, but it looked deserted, as if they'd left the cleaning up for tomorrow and gone to party somewhere else to-night.

Lorna looked back at the man sleeping on the grass. She couldn't leave him here and he was too big to drag home, even though she didn't live that far away. She could have gone to the sheriff's office, but she didn't want Jess to get into trouble. And she couldn't sit here all night hoping that someone would come along and help her out. No, she was going to have to deal with the man all by herself.

"Jess," she said aloud, inches from that handsome face. "Jess? Jess Sheridan, wake up." She tried shaking his shoulder, but she was too gentle. She spoke louder and shook harder and managed to get a muttered oath out of him before he went back to sleep. She supposed the amount he had drunk had more to do with his condition than the blow dealt by a pair of barbecue tongs, but she still felt responsible for his predicament. He'd tried to give her money. How sweet was that?

So Lorna kept talking and prodding until Jess Sheridan opened his eyes and said, "For God's sake, woman, leave me alone!"

Victory was hers, until she tried to get him to sit up, and then stand. He was heavy and sleepy and wobbly, but he put his arm around her when she told him to and she managed to lead him across the grassy park and across the street. There were lights on in most of the houses that lined the residential end of West Beaumont Street. They crossed Comstock without any problem, though Jess was a large man and Lorna was beginning to wonder if she had made a mistake in her plan of action. Screaming herself hoarse yelling for help might have been better than risking a broken back.

By the time she coaxed him up the three stairs to the front porch of her aunt's narrow yellow house, Jess had begun to walk under his own power.

"Where are we?" he asked when she settled him against the front of the house so she could get the key out of her pocket and unlock the front door.

"My house." She swung the door open and urged him to enter the living room.

"Why?"

"Because I couldn't leave you there in the park," she explained as she turned on a light. "Not after everything you did."

"Oh." He looked confused.

"How's your head feeling?"

"I'll live."

"I hope so." She smiled up at him. "I didn't know if I should take you to the hospital. I'd be glad to drive you home now if you'll tell me where you live."

He frowned and felt the back of his neck, then looked around the curtainless living room. Boxes were stacked neatly against the walls and the wood floor was bare. "Are you coming or going?"

"I just moved in," she said, and would have explained about her aunt and her job and probably blabbed the complete unabridged story of her life, but Jess began to sway again. She caught him before he toppled over, then hurried him to the bedroom off the living area, a room she hadn't had a chance to paint, and the only bed in the tiny house. Thank goodness she'd had time to make it this morning before leaving for the park.

"Sorry," he managed to say. "The wedding—the whiskey—" He stared at her as she pushed him backward against the pillows. "Funny hair," he muttered, touching one of the loose tendrils that had fallen on her cheek when she bent over. "Who *are* you?"

"Lorna," she replied. "And we may have to go to the hospital after all to get your head examined."

He grinned at her, making him look devilishly handsome and causing Lorna's heart to beat a tiny bit faster. "Honey, do I look crazy to you?"

He looked as if he belonged there, was her first thought. And then she caught herself. "You look like a man who has had too much to drink. Sleep it off and I'll drive you home later."

"Home," he repeated, then yawned. "Good idea," was the last thing he said before leaning back against the pillows and closing his eyes.

Lorna watched him for a moment and then decided he was asleep and would likely stay that way until she woke him to take him home. And she'd wake him, all right, as soon as she scrubbed off the barbecue sauce and washed her hair. She may have had a big crush on Jess Sheridan, star football player of the Marysville Marauders, when she was thirteen. She may have worshipped the rugged sheriff's deputy who didn't give her a speeding ticket the first day she got her driver's license, and she may have even secretly hoped that Jess wouldn't marry snippy Sue Miller, who didn't deserve him, and instead would notice that the girl down the street had grown up.

But she didn't expect him to remember her, even if tonight he was actually in her bed. Aunt Carol would roll over in her grave at the very idea, since the elderly woman hadn't exactly thought a whole lot of men and had held very loud opinions on the kind of women who took men into their beds before their wedding days.

"Well, Aunt Carol," Lorna explained aloud as she headed toward the bathroom, "I'm sorry, but I didn't know what else to do with him."

HIS OWN SNORING woke him up. That, and the pain throbbing at the back of his neck. Jess opened his eyes and expected to be in his motel room, but his motel room didn't smell like vanilla and hadn't been shared with a woman. And there was definitely a woman curled up in the bed beside him. He was afraid to move for fear of waking her up, but his eyes gradually adjusted to the darkness and he saw a faint light at the other end of the room that he hoped led to a bathroom.

He lifted the sheet and saw that he was fully dressed, which only added to his confusion. When he slid out of the bed, he knocked over his boots. The noise didn't appear to bother the woman, though. She lay curled away from him, long curly hair covering most of her face, her body relaxed and quiet.

Jess managed to find the bathroom and, realizing he smelled like someone had spilled booze all over him, took advantage of the pink-tiled shower and some vanilla-scented soap. He found mouthwash on the counters, towels in a narrow closet behind the door, and aspirin in the medicine cabinet above the sink. And since he didn't know where he was and didn't particularly care about it in the middle of the night, Jess went back to the bedroom—and found the sleeping woman sprawled across his side of the bed.

Who was she? He remembered a wedding. Jake's wedding. But he was a little fuzzy about the rest of the day and night leading up to being in bed with a beautiful blonde. He wasn't sure whether or not to untie the pink bath towel from around his waist and climb into bed with her, or if he should put his clothes back on and get the hell out of town.

If he knew what town he was in. The throbbing in his head lessened, but Jess figured he was better off staying where he was, which—before he woke—was in bed with Blondie here, if he could get back into it without waking her up.

His body definitely awakened the moment he touched her. Oh, he didn't mean to make getting into bed an erotic experience, but he couldn't explain that to the part of his body that reacted the moment he kneeled on the bed and attempted to scoot Blondie over a couple of inches. She moved easily, curling on her side again. She wore something soft, something with little flowers on it, and her arms were bare.

And her skin was soft. So soft that Jess dropped his towel on the floor and decided that the woman—whoever she was—must have invited him here, into her bed, and he damn well was not putting his jeans back on. He'd be a gentleman—or die trying—but he wasn't going to be uncomfortable. He'd never be able to get his pants over his erection now anyway.

Jess adjusted the pillows, slid under the soft, clean sheet and tried to get comfortable in the small bed. Trouble was, the woman's bottom curved against his thigh. And he had no place for his right hand, unless he put it over his head.

It wasn't easy to relax, and when the woman

turned over and pressed her nose into his rib cage, relaxing became downright impossible.

"Honey," he muttered, lowering his arm in an attempt to move her before she tickled him again. His fingers touched soft curls and ended up brushing them off her face. And what a face. Skin as soft as flower petals, delicate bone structure, lips soft against his body. Jess didn't know what to do with her, but his body was sure trying to explain it to him.

Selfish bastard. His ex-wife's words mocked him. Was it selfish to seduce a sleeping woman? He'd tried it—once—with Sue and had been thoroughly chewed out for it the next morning. No, he decided, removing his hand from Blondie's silky hair. He'd keep his hands—and his erection—to himself unless this woman woke up and told him—

"Nice," she said, and kissed him right above the rib he'd broken when, as a seven-year-old, he had fallen off a horse he wasn't supposed to ride. His rib had never felt better than when her mouth touched it. In fact, Jess thought his headache disappeared, too. Along with his reluctance.

He turned slowly onto his side, wishing she'd awaken. Hoping that when she opened her eyes she wouldn't look shocked and start screaming. She snuggled against him, her hand going around his waist, her elbow grazing what was rapidly becoming painfully aroused.

"Honey," he tried, wishing he could remember her name.

"Mmm," was all she said, lifting her face to his. Nope, her eyes were still closed. Maybe she liked to have sex with her eyes closed, he speculated. If so, he was more than ready to oblige. So he bent down and kissed her. Those full lips of hers were warm and obliging, so he kept kissing her. He moved closer, his thighs against her cotton-covered body. She didn't seem to mind, even seemed to be enjoying it, so Jess moved his free hand to the dip of her waist, and then to her nicely rounded thigh, to take the hem of her gown and lift it above her waist. Then he ran his hand along the curve of satiny skin and resisted the urge to take her right then. He didn't want to rush.

He hadn't had a woman in over a year. And he certainly didn't anticipate beginning a hot sex life when he arrived in Huntsville Monday, so Jess wanted to slowly and thoroughly make love to this sweet thing as if she was the last woman he'd have in a long, long time.

And she didn't seem to mind, either, come to think of it, when he lifted his lips from her mouth and down to her neck. He moved the nightgown higher, to expose one lovely shadowed breast to the dim light of the room. He couldn't resist cupping it with his hand, tasting the budded tip with his tongue, gently urging the woman onto her back so he could give the other breast the same attention. He heard her moan, and her fingers smoothed his shoulders and tickled his neck. He lifted his head and saw her smile, her eyes still closed. But he knew she was awake, or awake enough to know that he was making love to her now.

"Jess?" she whispered, and he surprised himself with how relieved he was that she knew his name, knew who was in her bed.

"Yes, honey," he replied, but her body tempted him once again, so he kissed a trail to her belly button, and lower. She was sweet and responsive when he touched her with his fingers, and when he eased her thighs apart and tasted her with his lips and tongue, he felt her shiver and heard her sigh. And wanted to be inside of her more than he wanted to breathe.

So Jess eased alongside of her and, as they lay facing each other, he fitted himself against her. She wrapped her arms around his neck, slid one leg over his, and welcomed him inside of her. He thought he'd died and gone to heaven—a heaven where a passionate woman wanted to make love with him.

Jess took his time, moving in and out slowly. Then deeper, testing to see if his length would hurt her. If anything, she seemed to want more of him, lifting her mouth to his to kiss him while they were joined together. He cupped her buttocks, holding her tightly against him as he took her again and again, until Jess wondered if he would ever want to do anything else but be inside of her. At the same time her breath caught, he felt the contractions of her climax and she made the tiniest of sounds against his mouth. That was all he needed to push him over the edge and when he came, it was for longer than he'd thought was humanly possible.

Much later, when dawn lightened the room and he slipped out of the bed to find his clothes, Jess made his escape. The woman was still asleep and Jess knew that, despite drinking too much last night, he'd managed to wind up in bed with Texas Tom's waitress. How that happened, he didn't remember, but he knew he wasn't going to stick around to find out. He had a job to get to. And, besides, women were never as nice to him in the morning as they were at night.

3

"SHERIDAN'S BACK," Lorna heard someone at the counter announce. "Carter said he walked into the sheriff's office late last night and moved his stuff in."

"Where's he been?"

"Workin' over in Huntsville, I heard. He was pretty broken up about that divorce," another man added. "Had to leave town, y'know, 'cuz she ran off with—who'd she run off with?"

No one answered, which Lorna found a little disappointing. She would have liked to know exactly what happened to Jess's marriage and why. She waited for someone to mention whether or not he had children, but no one offered the information.

"I heard he's renting a place from Jackson."

"Nah," came another opinion. "He won't live in town. He'll go out to his place and start ranchin' again."

"I thought his wife got the ranch," someone added. "You know, in the divorce."

"She sold it," another retired cowboy declared. "She always was a hard one to like, but she was a good looker, all right."

Lorna picked up the coffee carafe and turned to refill cups along the counter. Ten stools, ten men, ten
coffee cups. And one topic of conversation: the return
of Jess Sheridan. Her hand shook a little as she made
her way down the counter. She'd hoped Jess Sheridan
would walk back into her life; she'd prayed he
wouldn't. It just depended on the day. And the
weather. And how much her feet hurt.

"You okay, Lorna?" one of the older men asked.
"Maybe you should rest a little."

"I'm fine," she insisted, not much for sympathy.
"You make your bed, you lie in it," was another one
of her mother's maxims. Lorna figured she'd made
herself quite a complicated bed, all right. And she
would lie in it without complaining.

"Can we get some more cream in here?" the next
guy asked, pushing the stainless steel creamer toward her.

"Sure." She finished refilling the mugs, replen-
ished the cream, rang up two transactions on the cash
register and glanced out the window three times, but
saw no one or nothing of any interest. January in
Beauville wasn't exactly the busy season, and the
breakfast rush was over. She enjoyed her job at the
Coffee Pot Café. The customers were, for the most
part, a pleasant and undemanding group. Her boss
believed in serving good food, kept the place spotless

and didn't mind when Lorna took a few minutes to rest whenever she grew tired.

She glanced at the clock above the door and saw that it was almost ten o'clock. There would be some time to sit down before the lunch rush began.

So Jess Sheridan was back in town. She'd read in the paper he'd accepted the job as sheriff. She'd also read he was some kind of hero, having risked his life doing undercover work at the Huntsville prison.

Lorna didn't care what kind of hero he was. She only wanted him to go away before he discovered she was having his baby.

NOTHING IN BEAUVILLE had changed in six months, Jess figured. He'd done his stint at Huntsville, added a healthy sum to his bank account and now could afford to contact Bobby Calhoun about buying back his ranch. Until then he was homeless, or pretty close, if he didn't count his room at the motel. He'd looked at a couple of apartments above the drugstore, but Jess wasn't ready to move in just yet.

He drove along Beaumont Street, along the north border of the park, and realized he hadn't set foot in town since the weekend of Jake Johnson's wedding. That was one night he hadn't forgotten. And probably never would. He hadn't touched a drop of alcohol since. He'd never been so stupid in his life, unless he counted his marriage.

But that night in July had been one hell of a night. He shouldn't be thinking about sex. He shouldn't be cruising the streets of Beauville looking for the sight of a curvaceous curly-haired blonde and trying to remember where she lived the night he slept there. He knew it was a small house not too far from the park, but the next morning pain, embarrassment and guilt had combined to make him unaware of his precise surroundings until he stumbled back to the Grange and found his truck parked around the corner. It hadn't been one of his best mornings.

Jess turned on Main Street and tried to forget what a fool he'd been that night last summer. He could sure use a cup of coffee and he wouldn't mind a little conversation, either. The Coffee Pot didn't look crowded, which suited Jess just fine. He didn't feel like talking.

And he didn't think talking would be possible when his mouth went dry at the sight of the woman from last summer sitting in the café. But was it her? Jess hesitated before taking a seat at a table by the door. The woman in a booth at the other end of the room sat with her back to him, a familiar mass of yellow curls twisted into a knot at the top of her head.

He didn't know if he wanted it to be her or not. For one thing, he wasn't sure she'd remember him. Which wasn't exactly a compliment to the lady. Or to himself. For another, it was damn embarrassing to come face-to-face with someone you'd only known for one night—and one sexual encounter.

But what an encounter.

Jess ordered coffee from Charlie, who'd come out of the kitchen to welcome him back.

"Is there anything else I can get you, Jess? Breakfast is on the house," the man offered.

"In that case, I'll have a couple of eggs over easy," Jess said, not wanting to hurt Charlie's feelings.

"We've missed you around here," the cook said, going back behind the counter to pour the coffee. He came back with an oversize mug he set in front of Jess. "Black, right?"

"Yeah," he said, glancing once more at the yellow curls in the back booth. "You remembered."

"Sure. You weren't gone *that* long."

"Are you the waitress now, too, Charlie?"

"Nah. She's taking a break. Holler if you need anything."

"Thanks." Jess took a sip of coffee and looked around the café. The place hadn't changed for as long as he remembered. Though he'd grown up outside of town, his father brought him here for breakfast every Saturday morning. He nodded at a couple of older men on their stools who swiveled at the counter toward him. He pretended he recognized them, accepted their "welcome back" and "good to see you again," but his gaze went more often to the woman at the end of the room. In fact, she was seated at the last booth before the rest rooms, so Jess decided it was time he answered nature's call. Or at least pretended to.

He slid out of the booth, left his hat on the table, and headed toward the far end of the restaurant. He couldn't see her when he passed, though he tried to look out of the corner of his eye. Jess went into the men's room and washed his hands, smoothed back his hair and looked at the fool in the mirror, who looked back at him as if he was the biggest idiot in Texas.

When he stepped out, he was conscious of his heart racing faster than usual, and his throat had gone dry again. And all because of the sight of yellow curls. His gaze went right to her, and he knew her right away, even though she had her head lowered and appeared to be reading a magazine.

"Excuse me," he said, pausing at the table. The profile, the petite nose, the hair—it had to be her. So when she turned and lifted her gaze to meet his, there was no doubt he'd found the woman he'd made love to last July. In fact, she blushed. And he thought his own face felt a little too warm, but then again, Charlie didn't care to use a whole lot of air-conditioning this time of year.

"Yes?"

It occurred to him that he didn't know her name. "Haven't we met?"

She looked straight into his eyes and lied. "No, I don't think so."

"Really." He looked at her until those blue eyes blinked once and then looked away to her magazine. "Are you sure?"

She glanced toward him once again. "I'm sorry," she said, but there was no regret in her voice. "I suppose I would have remembered."

"Yeah." Jess walked away, toward his cooling coffee and the plate of eggs that Charlie had just set at his table. She didn't remember him or she didn't want to. He supposed she was as embarrassed as he was about that night. He thanked Charlie for the eggs, then lowered his voice so the cook would have to lean closer. "Is that your waitress?"

Charlie chuckled. "Yeah. I saw you talking to her, Jess. How'd you make out?"

"Not too good."

"You're not the first man around here who's tried and failed, Jess. Don't take it too hard."

"What's her name?"

"Lorna," Charlie replied, and the name sounded familiar. Had he known her name that night? He had a vague recollection of a waitress uniform and a fight over garbage bags. There'd been a ruckus, and that was all he remembered until waking up to find himself in bed with the most beautiful woman he'd ever seen in his life. Lorna.

"Lorna what?"

"Walters. She's from Marysville, but she inherited her aunt's house here in town last summer." Charlie winked. "If you want to know anything else, you'll have to ask her."

He intended to, now that he'd found her. Surprisingly it hadn't taken very long. She knew who he was, but she didn't want to admit it. He would talk to her again, ask her out for dinner, maybe. Show her that he wasn't the combative drunk she'd known a few months ago. He was the town's sheriff now, after serving as a deputy in Marysville for more than ten years. He was well-respected, or at least he hoped he was.

Jess attacked his eggs, even though he didn't have much of an appetite. Lorna Walters didn't want to have anything to do with him. He should have guessed that his luck with women couldn't be anything but bad. Some guys were lucky—and some guys were better off staying home with their dog, their refrigerator and the remote control.

HE WAS A QUICK EATER and he didn't linger over his second cup of coffee, which meant Lorna didn't have to make her morning break last longer than it should. There was no way she was going to get out of the booth and show Jess Sheridan her new figure, even if it meant sitting there until sundown. Oh, she knew she couldn't avoid seeing him until March, when the baby was due, but she hoped to stall the inevitable for a while longer.

"You feelin' okay?" Charlie asked, when she stood behind the counter once again and poured herself a glass of ice water.

"Fine." She fixed a fresh pot of coffee, wiped down the counters and checked the napkin holders to make sure they were filled.

"The new sheriff was asking about you," Charlie said, grinning at her. She thought for a moment her heart stopped.

"What'd you tell him?"

"I told him your name, that's all. And if he wanted to know anything else he should ask you." The cook shook his head. "For a pregnant woman, you sure get asked out a lot. How come you don't go?"

Lorna attempted a laugh and smoothed her white blouse over her rounded abdomen. "I'll give you one guess."

"That baby's gonna need a father," the man warned. "And you're gonna need a husband."

"That would be nice, Charlie," she agreed, trying to keep her voice light. "Do you have anyone in particular in mind?"

A voice piped up from the end of the counter. "How about the son-of-a-bitch who did this to you?"

"He's not available, Mike," she told the old man. Mike Monterro lived alone, spent hours at the café and wasn't shy about pronouncing his opinions. He looked about ninety, with a weathered brown face and wiry gray hair that stuck up in patches on the top of his head. Lorna was still a little bit afraid of him.

"Hmmph," the man grumbled, frowning at Lorna's belly. "In my day women didn't go around having kids if they weren't married. The men married 'em and gave the kids a name."

"Have you ever been married, Mike?" She hoped to change the subject as fast as she could, before he delivered another opinion on her pregnancy.

"Yes, ma'am, and a sweeter woman you'd never meet. She could bake pies that would make a man weep, my Felicia could."

"What kind of pies?" She poured a fresh cup of coffee and placed it in front of him. Mike usually stayed for lunch, then went home to "get some work done." Or so he said. Lorna figured he took a nap.

"Apple, peach, rhubarb, you name it." He sighed. "Felly's been gone twenty-seven years now and I still miss those pies." He gave her a sharp look. "Do you bake pies, missy?"

"No. I never learned."

"Well," he said, nodding to himself. "That's your

problem. You learn to bake pies and mebbee you'll get yourself a man."

Lorna hid her sigh. Mike didn't know it, but Lorna would have baked a thousand pies if it meant that Jess Sheridan would fall in love with her. "I wish it was that simple, Mike," she said.

He shrugged and picked up his coffee cup. "It should be, missy, yessiree."

WALTERS. LORNA WALTERS. He'd grown up with a Walters family. They'd lived down the street. There might have been a daughter named Lorna, but he didn't remember. Jess tapped her name into the computer, but came up with nothing but her driver's license and her Beauville address. She wasn't wanted for anything, had no record of speeding tickets or infractions of any kind. At least he knew where she lived and could see if that was the house that matched his memory.

Or not. He could let it go, chalk it up to one of those "strangers in the night" happenings, one of those things that was better left in the past.

He didn't know why he couldn't. He told himself he needed to apologize. He told himself he needed to know what exactly happened that night—after all, he'd had a lump on the back of his head for a week. He told himself once again he was acting like a fool. But at seven-twelve Monday evening, Jess knocked at

1205 North Comstock and waited for Lorna to come
to the door.

Her eyes widened when she recognized him, but
she was behind the screen door and didn't open it.

"Yes, can I help you?"

"I'm Jess Sheridan," he said. "And we *have* met."
He paused, hoping he was going about this in the
right way. "I wanted to apologize for that evening."

"You don't have anything to apologize for," she
said, and he noticed she held a white bed pillow in
front of her. She wore a fluffy blue robe and her hair
was damp.

"This isn't a good time to drop by, I guess." He
waited, hoping she would invite him inside. It was
damn hard to talk while standing on the other side of
a door. He started to feel uneasy, like he was making
a big mistake.

"Not really," she agreed. "It's a little embarrassing.
How did you find the house?"

"I'm the sheriff," he said. "I got your name from
Charlie and the rest was easy."

"I know who you are. I knew who you were last
July, too."

Once again he felt an unaccustomed heat tinge his
face. "There isn't much I remember about that night.
I was hoping you could fill me in. How drunk was I?"

"You were a perfect gentleman," Lorna said. "You

helped me out of a jam and you got yourself conked on the head for it. So I brought you home to recover."

"To recover," he repeated, remembering the way she'd felt in his arms. He'd recovered just fine, and when he'd put himself inside of her he'd thought he'd found heaven. Now it was Lorna's turn to blush.

"Could we just forget about that night?" she asked, those big blue eyes imploring him to end the conversation. "Please? I don't expect you to believe me, but I don't pick up drunks and bring them home after work. You were the first."

"And I'm not usually a drunk," Jess said. "I guess that was an unusual night for both of us." He'd believe anything she told him, Jess realized. Including that the earth was flat, the sky green and the state of Texas bordered the Atlantic Ocean. But he still had the nagging sense that there was something more, something else she hadn't told him. He hadn't been a cop for all these years for nothing. He fingered the prickles on the back of his neck and remembered the lump. "Who hit me?"

"Texas Tom." She crushed the pillow tighter against her body and he could see her fingers digging into the fabric. "The Barbecue King. I was working for him during the wedding reception."

Jess struggled to remember. "Was there something about garbage?"

"Yes." She smiled, just a little. But it was enough to

make Jess's heart beat faster. He wished she'd smile at him all the time, wished she'd come out from behind the screen and invite him inside. "Tom wasn't behaving very well, and you defended me and made him give me the money he owed me for working at the wedding. I—uh—couldn't leave you lying there by the garbage, especially because I was the reason you were hurt in the first place."

That made sense. But what was she hiding? "I'd like to take you to dinner," he said, sounding as casual as he possibly could while he thought he might be having a heart attack. "To thank you for helping me out. And to apologize for not sticking around the next morning to, uh, thank you in person." There. He'd gotten all the words out, but it hadn't been easy. Not when he knew what that body felt like, or how heavy her breasts were in his hands. And how sweet she tasted when she parted her lips for his kiss.

"It's not necessary," she replied. "Honest."

"I'd like to anyway."

"I can't," she said. "But thank you for coming."

"Can't or won't?"

She looked startled. "What?"

"Are you involved with someone else?" He'd assess the competition for himself, Jess decided, ignoring a fierce stab of jealousy. He'd like to know if the other guy was worthy of her.

"Um, no. I'm not really going out with anyone right now."

"Then you're free to have dinner with me Friday night," Jess declared, figuring he'd put up with enough dillydallying around for one evening.

"Mr. Sheridan, I really can't go out with you."

"Call me Jess," he said. "I'll pick you up at seven." He turned quickly and went down the porch steps toward his vehicle. He didn't want to hear her objections, didn't want to hear her refuse his invitation. He would stay away from the Coffee Pot for the rest of the week so she wouldn't have a chance to tell him she couldn't go. If she called the sheriff's office, he would have Chelsea say he wasn't available.

He was a patient man. He could wait until Friday.

LORNA DIDN'T put the pillow down until the sheriff had driven off and she heard the engine fade down the street. Lucky for her she'd been making her bed when he knocked and had the pillow in her hand when she went to the door.

She couldn't keep it from him forever, of course. Maybe not even for another day. But Lorna wanted to delay that particular confrontation for as long as possible. She was a coward of the worst kind, and she hated conflict. There would be a scene. She hated scenes.

Lorna stood at the door and watched the kids

across the street play in their front yard. Something in the grass had caught their attention and the two oldest children appeared fascinated. The Bennetts were fun to watch, especially the toddler. Emily Bennett stepped outside, the little girl tucked against her hip, and told the others to go inside and take their baths. Lorna smiled at the look of disgust on the boy's face, but he did what he was told.

Emily glanced over toward her and waved, so Lorna waved back and the redheaded woman started across the street. "Lorna!" she called. "How are you?"

She swung the door open as Emily and Elly came up the steps. "I'm fine. Just very pregnant, that's all."

"Is everything okay?"

"Sure. Come on in." Visiting with Emily always made her feel like part of the neighborhood.

"I saw the new sheriff at your door and I wondered..." Emily's brows rose. "Do I sense a mystery here? You're blushing."

"I'm just a little warm, that's all," she fibbed, and turned her attention to the toddler. "Hi. Do I get a kiss?" The baby obliged with a loud smack that didn't land anywhere near Lorna's cheek, but Lorna thanked her.

"I have baby clothes for you," Emily announced. "I finally got George to go up in the attic and dig out the boxes."

"I appreciate that, but are you sure you won't be needing them?"

Emily grinned and perched on the arm of an over-stuffed chair. "You're a few months ahead of me. By the time I have this next baby, yours will have out-grown a lot of them."

"I'm wondering how to deal with *one* child," Lorna said. "I can't imagine four."

"It's easier if you don't have them all at once," her neighbor chuckled. "Do you know if you're having a boy or a girl?"

"Not yet. Some days I think I should ask the doctor and other times I'm glad I don't know. Is that silly?" She lowered herself onto the couch and smoothed the robe over her belly. "I suppose I should be a little more prepared."

"I have plenty of baby clothes for you," Emily assured her, "whether it's a boy or a girl. I'll just bring them all over and you can use what you want."

"I don't know how to thank you—"

"We'll trade baby-sitting some day," Emily said, keeping Elly from grabbing the leaves off Lorna's trailing ivy plant. She looked around the living room. "I see you've been painting."

"Aunt Carol loved pink and I'm still trying to get rid of it."

"The white's much nicer," Emily said before she stood. "I'd better go. You look like you're ready for bed. Are you going to keep working at the Coffee Pot much longer?"

"As long as I can," Lorna replied. "I have three more months before the baby comes, and I'm going to try to work right up until my due date."

She walked Emily to the door, waved goodbye to the toddler and then shut the door on the world. She had a job, she had a friend, and she was about to have a child. Jess Sheridan didn't fit into the picture anywhere at all.

4

"MISS LORNA WALTERS on the phone," Chelsea whispered, giving Jess a curious look. His new secretary, fresh out of business school, wore purple-painted fingernails two inches long and platinum blond hair that hung straight to her chin. He figured she spent hours on her makeup every morning, and she wore the shortest skirts he'd ever seen. Carter, the young deputy, could barely take his eyes off her when he came into the office, but Jess wished she'd lose the purple nails and stick to something more conservative. "You changed your mind yet?"

Jess prayed for patience. If the twenty-one-year-old hadn't scored the highest marks on the secretarial exam, she would never have gotten this job. It had become necessary to hire someone after Dot Jacobs retired when Matt Morrison decided he was ready to stop being sheriff and start traveling to visit his eleven grandchildren. Fortunately Chelsea Higgs was some kind of computer whiz and hadn't met a computer program she couldn't operate.

"No," he said. "Tell her I'm not available and don't offer to take a message."

The sheriff department's new secretary did as she was told, and then shook her head. "That's no way to handle women, Sheriff."

"Really," he said, hoping she would get the message that he didn't need romantic advice. Even if he did need romantic advice, Chelsea would not be the one he'd ask for it. She'd probably advise him to get a tattoo or shave his head.

She tapped his desk calendar with a purple fingernail. "You should be nicer. You have a date with her tomorrow night. She must be special."

"How'd you know I have a date with her?" He'd written "L at 7", nothing more.

"You wrote the appointment in red ink. You never use red ink."

"It's business," he lied.

"You don't work on Friday nights."

"We've worked together for four days, Chelsea," Jess pointed out. "You couldn't know much about my choice of pens, or my schedule." It irked him that she was right.

"Important things are written in red, phone calls in pencil and meetings in black. Why don't you ever use blue?"

"Chelsea," he warned, running out of patience. "Stay away from my calendar."

"Can't," she said, unperturbed by his growl. "I'm

putting your schedule into the computer so I can print out daily reminders."

"I don't need daily reminders." He turned back to the stack of paperwork on his desk. Like he would forget a dinner date with Lorna. He'd spent the past three days trying to figure out how to avoid seeing her, though the sight of the Coffee Pot Café made him slow down the patrol car and long for a glimpse of her. He'd be fine, he told himself, once he'd apologized. Once he'd shown her who he really was, a respectable member of society and a sober dinner partner.

"Sure you do," Chelsea insisted. "I have a great software program for it. Are you going to bring her flowers?"

"No."

"Why not?"

"I don't want to make a big deal out of this," he told her. "It's just dinner. With an old friend."

"This is the same Lorna Walters who's the pretty blond waitress at the Coffee Pot, right?"

"How'd you know that?"

Chelsea shrugged. "She's the only person named Lorna in town. So you see? I know lots of things. Besides, you left the report you got on her on your desk."

Jess made a mental note to keep his private paperwork locked in his desk drawer.

"So," she continued, "if she's such an old friend and you're taking her out to dinner, why aren't you taking her phone calls?"

"Because I don't want to give her a chance to turn me down."

"Hmm. You're not exactly the overconfident type," she mused. "So you have the hots for her. Has this been going on a long time?"

"Don't be crude, Chelsea." He pointed to a large stack of manila folders. "Those need to be filed."

She ignored him. "Does she have the hots for you, too, or is this a first date?"

"First date." His first in four and a half years.

"With Lorna Walters," Chelsea added, as if making sure she was right about the name. "If you want to make a good impression, you'd better bring flowers." Chelsea looked at him as if she wanted to ask him another question, but the phone ringing interrupted her and she had to turn away to answer it. "For you," she said, punching the button that transferred the call to his desk on the other side of the room. "There's a problem at the saloon."

"Tell them I'll be right over."

"Jake Johnson wants to talk to you first," she said, so Jess picked up the receiver and greeted his old friend.

"What's going on?"

"It's Bobby Calhoun again. He's drunk as a skunk

and just rode his horse through the front door. I think the boys out at the ranch have been watching old western videos," Jake explained. "I happened to be in town and saw him, so I'm trying to calm down the bartender and get Bobby out of here before he causes too much trouble."

"I'll be right there," Jess promised. "He doesn't have a gun, does he?"

"No, he's not that stupid."

"Good." He hung up the phone and told Chelsea where he was going.

"Okay," she said, examining her fingernails as if she was admiring their strange color. "What kind of flowers should I get?"

He paused halfway out the door. "Flowers?"

"For your date tomorrow night. If you don't order something ahead, you'll be stuck getting one of those bouquets at the supermarket."

"No flowers," Jess told her, but as he strode outside to his vehicle he wondered if he should follow her advice. Chelsea was a woman, after all—barely. She had some strange beauty ideas, but still...he ought to think about flowers. He didn't know why it mattered so much, but it did. He didn't remember a lot about that night they spent together, but he did remember the lovemaking. He'd remember that night 'til the day he died.

"YOU'RE AS NERVOUS as a cat near water, Lorna." Charlie set two luncheon specials on the serving counter. "You okay?"

"I'm fine." Okay? She was six months pregnant and her date was going to show up at her door in three hours. Her very unwanted date. She picked up the plates and took them to the two ladies at table six, the same ladies who came for a late lunch every Friday. "Here you go," she said, setting the plates of fish and chips in front of them. "Enjoy."

"Oh, we will," the older one said. "And how are you feeling, Lorna?"

"Bigger and bigger all the time," she said, trying to smile. Instead she felt her eyes fill up with tears, and she turned away before the ladies could offer any sympathy that would make her sob like a two-year-old.

She hadn't seen him all week, though the day after Jess showed up at the café, she'd jumped every time the bell on the door jangled to announce another customer and braced herself to face the questions that would certainly follow. He'd stayed away, so yesterday she realized he wasn't going to give her a chance to turn down his invitation. She'd even called the sheriff's office, which hadn't gotten her anywhere. Jess Sheridan was going to show up at her door tonight the way he had promised.

By four o'clock she was finished for the day, so she

left through the back door, unlocked her car, which she sometimes parked in the small lot behind the building, and drove home. Emily, pulling weeds from her garden, waved as Lorna pulled up in her driveway, so Lorna walked across the street to say hello.

"You look like you need a friend," her neighbor said. "Want a cup of coffee?"

"I don't want to interrupt—"

"Interrupt gardening? Please," Emily laughed, and stood. "I hate gardening." She stripped off her gloves and tossed them to the ground. "George took the kids to pick out a video for tonight, so we have the house to ourselves for a few minutes."

Lorna followed Emily around the side of the house and into the kitchen, but she didn't sit down right away. "Emily, how pregnant do I look?"

"As in months?"

"Yes."

Emily tilted her head and studied Lorna's belly. "I guess it depends on what you wear, but right now, in that uniform, you look about six months along. You have one of those basketball pregnancies, so—"

"Basketball pregnancy?"

"You know, when it looks like you stuck a basketball under your blouse. Your basketball is pretty small right now, but you're wearing that maternity uniform, so it's really not showing much. Why?"

Lorna sat down and eyed her stomach. Her small basketball pushed against the cotton fabric of her skirt. "Someone wants to take me out to dinner tonight."

Emily grinned. "You have a date? Good for you."

"He doesn't know I'm pregnant."

Her friend forgot about making coffee and sat down at the table across from Lorna. "Wait a minute. You met him on the *Internet?*"

"No. I don't have a computer. I met him at the Johnson wedding." She didn't elaborate; Emily didn't need to know the details of her neighbor's mistake.

"Lorna, honey, he's going to be able to tell," Emily said, her expression still amused. "He's going to be surprised when he discovers his date is wearing a maternity dress." She paused. "Do you *have* a maternity dress?"

Lorna nodded. "One."

"Good. I'd offer to loan you one of mine, but you're a lot smaller than I am. And they're not in very good shape after three pregnancies." Emily propped her head up with her elbow and gave Lorna a searching look. "You're pretty upset about this. You can still say no."

"He's pretty stubborn." He would show up on her doorstep promptly at seven and he would look at her as if he wanted to devour her and then his gaze would drop to her abdomen and he would guess this baby was his. Or not, she mused. Men didn't know much about pregnancy and he might believe any story she might tell him. And then she'd have turned herself into an unwed pregnant liar.

"You can still say 'no, my feet are swollen' or something," Emily declared. "Unless you like the guy and you're really hungry for dinner."

"I like the guy," she admitted. "I've had a crush on him since I was thirteen. And these days I'm always hungry."

"Then what's the problem?"

"We've never been out on a date before." Lorna patted her tummy. "My little basketball is going to scare him to death." And he might wonder if it's his and cause all sorts of complications. Which he had a right to, she amended, trying to be fair.

"If it's too uncomfortable, you can always end the evening before you order appetizers. Or when he shows up at your door you can tell him you've changed your mind."

"Once he sees the real me, he's going to back up and fall down the porch steps."

"Maybe not," Emily said, but she didn't sound convinced. "Not if you've known each other for years."

"He doesn't remember me," Lorna explained, smiling despite her nervous stomach. "I was the girl who lived down the street and admired him from afar."

"Well, you're going to see him up close tonight." Emily's gaze went to Lorna's belly. "If you wear something loose enough, he might think you've just gained weight."

"Wishful thinking," she replied, at the same instant the back door opened and Emily's children tumbled into the kitchen. The ensuing chaos—as the two older children both talked at once, the baby demanded her mother and George good-naturedly complained about the decision-making process at the video store—ended their conversation.

"Good luck," Emily whispered a few minutes later, when Lorna moved toward the door.

"Thanks."

"Let me know how it goes?"

"Oh, you'll know. If you look out your window at seven-oh-five, you'll see him running back to his car," Lorna promised. Emily laughed, but Lorna hadn't been joking.

She went home to her depressingly quiet house, with its half-painted, half-furnished living room and a bedroom that reminded her of that one night with Jess. She'd been foolish to bring him home, even more foolish to put him into her bed. She'd been so bone-wrenching tired that night, so tired she'd crawled into bed with him because there was no other place to sleep but the wood floor.

She should have known better, she told herself as she headed for her pink-tiled bathtub. He'd touched her and kissed her and she'd melted against him as if she belonged with him, skin to skin, mouth to mouth. She'd been too sleepy to think of birth control, too aroused to think of anything but that Jess Sheridan was making love to her.

Maybe, with luck, he wouldn't remember a thing about it.

JESS TRIED TO REMEMBER what to do on a date. He hadn't been out with anyone but his wife so he was out of practice. They would go out to dinner, but then what? A movie? The only thing playing was a war movie he'd seen in Huntsville two weeks ago. Dancing? Well, he wasn't much of a dancer, but it would be a good excuse to hold her in his arms.

No, he wanted to avoid any physical stuff. He didn't want her to think he was trying to get back in her bed on the first date. Not that he'd mind, but the point of this whole damn silly dinner idea was...what? Damned if he knew now, except he couldn't wait to see her again.

He'd thought about her all day. Thought about impressing her with food and wine and dessert. Chelsea said not to forget to order dessert and to offer to share anything she was thinking about choosing, but then not to eat much of it and let her have it all, especially if it was chocolate. Jess stopped at the gift and floral shop on Main Street and picked up the flowers Chelsea had insisted on ordering.

He felt like an idiot, especially when the gray-haired woman behind the counter winked at him, told she'd added extra "baby's breath"—whatever the hell that was—to the bouquet and wished him a nice evening.

Nice? He was going to spend the evening wishing he was in bed with her. He was going to spend the next two, three, four hours trying not to touch her, not to scare her off. He didn't know why he turned into a lust-crazed maniac each time he saw her, but he should damn well be able to get over it. His years of marriage should have cured him of making another mistake. His divorce had proved he could get over anything he set his mind to.

Lorna answered the door after the first knock and she pushed the screen door toward him to let him in. "Come in," she said, and he thought she sounded almost as nervous as he felt.

"Thanks." He took off his Stetson and noticed she'd worn her curly hair long tonight, with the sides pulled back off her face with sparkly barrettes. She turned away from him and led him over to the living room area. He vaguely remembered the room and had the impression it had been empty when he was last here.

"Would you like a drink? Whiskey and soda? Beer? Pop?"

"Whiskey and soda, thanks." She wore a dark blue dress made out of some floaty fabric, and her hair cascaded down her back. He didn't remember it being that long, but he liked it. Her back was toward him as she left the kitchen, and then he remembered the flowers. He'd left them in the car.

"I'll be right back," he called, and raced out the door, down the steps and to his car. The young woman across the street, a little kid attached to her hip, watched him curiously, probably thinking there was some police emergency. He retrieved the flowers—yellow roses with lots of little white flowers surrounding them—and headed back to Lorna's front door, where he let himself in and returned to the living room.

She stood in the hall watching him, his drink in her hand. He couldn't identify the expression on her face, but he knew she was the loveliest woman he'd ever seen.

"These are for you," Jess said, noting the surprised expression cross her face. Her blue eyes lit up with pleasure as she traded his drink for the flowers and, for only a second, touched his suddenly shaking hands.

"They're beautiful." Lorna didn't look as though she had expected flowers, which pleased him. "I'm sure you don't remember, but your mother used to let me pick flowers in her garden."

"My mother?"

"We lived down the street from you in Marysville."

"So you *are* that Walters. I couldn't remember—" his gaze dropped lower to note that the dress she wore was pretty big, as if it belonged to someone else—or else Lorna had gained weight "—if they had a daughter or not."

"I'll put these in water," she said, and turned to hurry away, through the living room to the kitchen. He didn't remember the kitchen, had a vague memory of a pink bathroom and a bedroom with nothing in it but a bed.

He returned to the living room, to sink into the beige loveseat and sip his whiskey. He guessed she didn't think he was a drunk or she wouldn't have offered it to him. She seemed to be gone a long time, but when she returned she carried a large white vase filled with his flowers, which she set on a flat-topped trunk between them before she perched on the edge of an overstuffed chair covered with faded flowers.

"So," he said, wishing he'd planned what he was going to say. "Are you hungry?"

"Yes, but—"

"But?" He frowned at her. For some reason she looked guilty. Definitely guilty. "You're going to back out?"

"As you can see, I'm not exactly dating right now."

Good, he wanted to say, not that he wanted to get involved with a woman again. But he sure didn't like the idea of Lorna going out with just anybody. "Why not?"

She gave him an odd look, almost as if she thought he was joshing her. "No particular reason," she eventually replied, but the look on her face didn't change. She really was one of the most beautiful women he'd ever seen, Jess realized.

"I made reservations at the Steak Barn," he said. Now he wished he had planned to drive to Marysville instead, to someplace more intimate and where they wouldn't be interrupted by everyone in town. He wore his pager, but he sure as hell hoped that Carter could handle anything that came up. The kid was eager enough and Jess figured he secretly longed for a crime wave.

"For what time?"

He glanced at his watch. "Seven-thirty." This wasn't going well. Next thing he knew he'd be talking about the weather, which was damn boring. "Tell me about Texas Tom. How did you end up working for him?"

"I answered an ad in the paper. I'd lost my job in

Dallas and decided to come back here when my aunt left me this house."

"And you'd just moved in last July?"

"You remembered the boxes. Yes, the house was pretty empty."

Except for the bed, he remembered. Jess took another sip of his drink. She really was wearing the strangest dress. He didn't know what he'd expected. Something tighter. With a short skirt. Like a waitress outfit only in a different color. That would have looked nice. "What did you do in Dallas?"

"I was an assistant buyer at Neiman Marcus, but they downsized and that was that."

"From Neiman Marcus to Texas Tom is a pretty big jump."

"Dallas to Beauville is, too," she answered, giving him one of her heart-stopping smiles. He wanted to haul her off to her bedroom and see if the passion he remembered so vividly was actually real.

"Yeah," was all he could come up with. He swallowed hard and took another sip of his drink. The lady bought good whiskey.

"I only worked for Tom for that one day. Then Charlie offered me the waitressing job and I took it. I'd waitressed in college, so I knew what I was doing."

"Do you miss Dallas?" *Are you going to leave here and go back to the city?* he wanted to know.

"Not really. I guess I'm a small-town girl at heart, even if I do have a closet full of expensive shoes."

The dress looked expensive, too, he noted. So maybe it was meant to hide her figure and discourage men from jumping her. Maybe she'd worn it to discourage him. The thought annoyed him.

"We'd better go," Jess said a little abruptly. He finished his drink in one swallow, set the glass down on the trunk top and stood.

"All right." She got up from her chair and turned to pick her purse off a little table nearby.

That's when he saw it. The outline of her abdomen. The curve of her belly. The unmistakable shape of...pregnancy? Lorna Walters was in the middle of having a baby. No wonder she didn't date much these days. Jess looked away and strode to the door before he said anything stupid, like *who the hell is he?* and *what were you doing with someone else?* or *do you love him?* or *do you want me to arrest him for you?*

"Jess?" She came up behind him.

"What?" He turned and kept his gaze on her face. She looked uncertain and very, very vulnerable.

"You don't have to do this," she said.

"Do what?" Of all the things he anticipated tonight, discovering that Lorna was pregnant was never on the list.

"Go out to dinner. I already told you how you

ended up here and you know about Texas Tom hitting you, so there really isn't anything else to—"

"You said you were hungry," he interrupted. He frowned down at her, unwilling to give her a chance to end the evening before it began.

"Are you?"

Did she realize he'd noticed she was very pregnant? He wasn't going to back out, not when he had something to prove. "Yes," he said, then louder, "Yes."

"Well, it would be nice to be waited on for a change," she admitted, her voice soft, the way he liked it.

"Then let's get out of here," he said, holding the door open for her. From the back she didn't look pregnant. "I hope you like steak." He'd never dated a pregnant woman before, hadn't even been around too many of them. He didn't know if they ate special stuff or what.

"I do," she said. "I've never been to the Steak Barn."

He felt clumsy and awkward, but he settled her in the passenger seat of the county's Ford Tahoe and hoped for the best. Maybe he could pretend he didn't notice, like a gentleman pretended he didn't notice when a lady had a run in her stocking or lipstick on her teeth.

Jess drove to the Steak Barn and tried not to think

about Lorna's future child. Where the hell was the father? He thought for a split second—and only for a split second—that the child could be his, but he wouldn't have been foolish enough to take a chance like that. Besides, he and Sue had never had kids, though they'd tried hard enough those first years. He'd heard she and her new husband had had a baby last month, so not getting pregnant was one more thing to add to the list of Things That Were His Fault.

"It's a lovely evening," Lorna said into the silence.

So they were talking about the weather now. Well, Jess thought, it sure beat the hell out of talking about babies. "Yeah," he said. "Nice."

5

LORNA WAITED for the question, but throughout dinner Jess pointedly ignored the fact that she looked pregnant. Instead he asked her about Dallas. And her home in Marysville.

"I lived in the blue house on the corner," she explained. "My mother and father taught square dancing all over this part of the state. They loved to dance."

"And you?"

"I have two left feet," she admitted. "Much to their disappointment I wasn't very musical either. They tried to give me all sorts of lessons—even the steel guitar—but I was hopeless."

"Do they still live there?"

"My father does. Mom died a few years ago and Daddy still belongs to a group and dances every weekend. He still calls square dances too, though there isn't as much demand for it as there used to be." The waitress came and cleared their dinner plates, then promised to be back with the dessert menu. "What about your family?"

"My older sister's in Austin. She's trying to be the next Shania Twain, or at least that's what she tells me. Do you remember her?"

"Vaguely." She'd been more entranced with Jess, the tall quiet boy who always treated her as an equal whenever their paths had infrequently crossed. He was already in high school when she was picking flowers in his mother's garden, but once he helped her dig up a rosebush his mother had given her. And she watched him out her bedroom window when he drove to school each day. She'd always thought of him as hers, so it came as a shock when she graduated from high school and learned he was engaged to someone else.

The waitress, an older lady who looked as if she'd been working at the Steak Barn all her life, plopped the dessert menus in front of them. "Y'all want coffee?"

"Tea, please," Lorna said.

"Sheriff, what about you?"

"Coffee, thanks, Pat."

"Anything for you, honey," she said, and smiled as if the sun just came out. "You want the usual?"

Lorna looked at him. "What's 'the usual'?"

"Apple pie," he admitted. "I've eaten here a lot since I moved back. But I think I'll skip it tonight and just have coffee. Not decaf, the real stuff."

"You think I'd give a police officer decaf coffee?"

Pat eyed Lorna. "What about you, honey? How about the chocolate mousse cake or a nice piece of peanut butter ice cream pie? You have any cravings yet?"

Lorna ignored the question and looked at Jess. "You're not having any dessert?"

"Order what you want and we can share, if you like."

"All right." She turned to Pat. "The apple pie, with whipped cream. I want to see if it's better than what we serve at the Coffee Pot."

"That's why you looked familiar. I worked there, too, when I was younger and could get up that early in the morning. Tell Charlie I said hi."

"I will," Lorna promised, then wondered if Jess was deliberately avoiding the subject of her pregnancy or if he was just blind. "Do you wear contacts?"

"No." He gave her an odd look. "Why?"

"Just wondering." So he was intentionally ignoring the size of her abdomen. She didn't know if that made tonight easier or not. Didn't he wonder if he had anything to do with it? Or was he truly unaware that they'd made love that night? He looked at her sometimes as if he remembered, all right. Like now. He was looking at her as if he wanted to kiss her, and she wished he would. She would like to be kissed by him again. "What about your parents? What are they up to these days?"

"They sold the house, bought an Airstream trailer and travel all over the country."

"That sounds like fun."

"It's a little strange," he said, "but I'm getting used to getting postcards from places I've never heard of."

Lorna shared the pie, drank her tea, talked about Beauville. She told him waitress stories; he told her tales of his days as a young and naive deputy sheriff. She didn't ask about his ex-wife or the divorce, but she would have listened if he wanted to tell her about it. He didn't.

"Jess," she began, when there was a lull in the conversation.

"I think Jake Johnson and his wife just walked in," he said, his attention focused over her shoulder to the entrance of the restaurant.

"Oh." She thought she would tell him, had worked up her courage to tell him she was going to have a baby. She didn't want to tell him this was his child. Unless he asked, of course, and then she wouldn't lie. He deserved to know, but did he want to? Maybe he was one of those people who didn't want to know, and therefore wouldn't have to deal with the problem. Lorna didn't like thinking of her baby as "the problem," though. She certainly didn't want Jess to feel that way either.

The Johnsons appeared at their table to be introduced to Lorna, who told them she was at their wedding serving barbecued ribs.

"We must make it up to you," Elizabeth said. She was radiant and she held her husband's hand as if she never wanted to let it go. "You'll have to come out to the ranch for dinner sometime. I'm learning how to cook, so you'd better be brave."

"Thanks for the help yesterday," the tall rancher told Jess. "I sure didn't want to see Bobby land in jail."

"Did he sober up?"

"Eventually. Dusty Jones is the new foreman, and he's got his hands full." Jake turned to Lorna. "It's nice to see you someplace besides the café. I didn't know you two knew each other," he said, giving Jess a curious look. "You've been in town for five days and you already have a date with the prettiest lady in Beauville."

"We met at your wedding," Jess replied. "Would you like to sit down and have a drink?"

Elizabeth blushed. "Oh, I can't drink right now."

Lorna knew exactly what the woman meant. "Congratulations?"

"Yes," the woman admitted. "How smart you are!"

"When are you due?"

"June twenty-first," she said, beaming. "We didn't

want to tell anyone until I made it through the first trimester. I guess I was a little superstitious about it."

Jess stood and shook Jake's hand. "Congratulations, Jake." He bent over and kissed Elizabeth's cheek. "I couldn't be happier for the two of you."

"Sit down and finish your coffee," Jake said. "We're going to find a quiet corner, have dinner and argue over baby names."

Lorna wanted to say she had a book of baby names at home that the couple could borrow, but she kept silent. Elizabeth wouldn't have known she was pregnant, though Jake would have noticed. He was in the café whenever he had errands to do in town, but Lorna didn't remember seeing Elizabeth there. "Congratulations again," she said, and watched the couple head for a corner booth, hand in hand. Then she looked back at her date. Surely the topic of babies would lead to questions of his own, but the man kept silent.

Very silent.

She excused herself to go to the ladies' room, which fortunately was behind her. At least she didn't have to walk past him, her belly on the same level as his nose. Once she was in the privacy of the ladies' room, she blinked back tears—those damn tears came way too easily these days—and wondered once again if she should bring up the subject herself. *By the way, I'm pregnant*, she could say. *Did you see that I resemble a kangaroo? Notice anything different from the last time you saw me?*

No, not that one. The last time he saw her she was naked in bed beside him. She wished he hadn't left without saying goodbye. The coward had bailed out at dawn's early light and hadn't been seen again. She supposed he was embarrassed; Lord knew she certainly was. And then she'd discovered he'd had a job in Huntsville and wasn't expected back in Beauville until January, when he would take over for Matt Jacobs at the beginning of the year. She'd waited, telling herself it didn't matter if he didn't remember. She remembered. She always would.

Well, if he wasn't going to say anything, she wasn't going to say anything. This gave her more time to decide what to tell him and made her feel less guilty for not telling him sooner.

Lorna splashed some water on her face and dried her skin with a paper towel. There. She looked presentable, at least for someone carrying around a little human being who liked to kick his mommy every time she sat down for more than five minutes.

She would tell the man nothing. The stupid sheriff would have to figure it out for himself.

HE LET HIS BREATH OUT the minute Lorna left the table. It felt damn good to breathe again, because he'd been on edge since he'd caught on the woman was going to have a baby. Meaning there had been someone else before him.

And he still wanted her. He must be some kind of pervert, lusting after a pregnant woman. He glanced over his shoulder to where Jake sat next to Elizabeth. But there was a man in love with his pregnant wife and who looked like he wanted to make love to her, so maybe he wasn't a pervert after all. Jess had heard they'd met when she and her niece came out to visit the Dead Horse Ranch last summer. Jess would have bet a month's salary that there had been no one-night stand in their past to complicate things.

Jess looked down at the empty dessert plate in the middle of the table. They'd gotten all the way through dessert and he still hadn't managed to apologize to her for that night. That was the reason for this whole date to begin with. That, and wanting her to like him and see that he wasn't normally a fool.

She returned from the ladies' room too soon, before he figured out what he was going to say next.

"Would you like anymore to drink?" was all he could think of.

"No, thank you." She was polite and sweet and about as obtainable as the moon. She belonged to someone else, he told himself. She was having his child. "Tell me about the Johnsons," she said, as if she was really interested. "Have you known them long?"

"Jake's my age. We played football in high school.

I used to own a ranch near the one where he used to work. Now he and Elizabeth have their own place south of town."

"Is Elizabeth from around here?"

"No. She's from back East somewhere." He drained the rest of his coffee and wondered if it was time to take Lorna home. "I guess we should go."

"All right." He thought she might have looked disappointed, but he figured he must have imagined it. He'd tried real hard to make sure she had a good time, but he was no master of small talk or dinner conversation. She'd looked like she was enjoying herself, but maybe that was because she liked the food. She'd eaten every bite of her small steak, baked potato and broccoli. She'd given him most of the pie, but he knew she'd liked that, too.

He had redeemed himself, so why was he sorry the evening was over?

Ten minutes later he walked her up the stairs to her front door. She found her key in her purse and unlocked the door before turning to smile up at him. "Thank you for dinner," Lorna said.

"Thank you for rescuing me at the wedding reception." He watched her cheeks turn pink and worried that he shouldn't have brought that up again.

"You don't owe me anything. You helped me with Texas Tom, so it was the other way around, remember?"

He didn't think so, not if his foggy memory was any indication. It probably would be rude to apologize for making love to her, especially if he didn't regret it for one second.

Jess paused, then leaned over and kissed her cheek. "Good night."

"Good night." She opened the door and slipped inside, leaving Jess on the porch to decide that he had done his duty; from now on he would leave this woman alone. She had her life and he had his.

The thought depressed him.

LORNA WATCHED the sheriff's car drive away before she sank onto her couch and leaned back against the cushions. Her back hurt and she had to get up at five, but she wasn't the least bit sleepy. She kicked off her shoes, wriggled her bare toes and rested her feet on the coffee table. The baby executed a couple of somersaults, making her smile.

"Your daddy's not very bright," she told her abdomen. "But that's okay. I don't think he wants to be a daddy right now."

She'd always thought she loved Jess, since she was thirteen and he was the handsomest boy she'd ever seen. She'd grown up thinking that no matter what, he would be hers. His marriage disappointed her, but she decided she'd outgrown her childhood crush and had a couple of boyfriends in college. While working in Dallas, she heard about his divorce, but it wasn't until that night of the wedding that she'd realized just how much he still mattered to her.

Their lovemaking had been a surprise, something to treasure as a special memory. But now she knew firsthand unexpected passion often led to other surprises, such as the little being inside of her now.

"Don't worry," she whispered. "I'll love you enough for him *and* for me."

A SOFT HAND TOUCHED HIS WAIST, tickled his skin in an alarmingly arousing way. He shifted, wanting to make love to her. His arousal was almost painful, evidence of his re-action to having that sweet-smelling female snuggled up against him. Somehow he managed to lift away her tangled nightgown, which left him access to the most inviting body he'd ever had the privilege to touch.

He didn't know who she was, though her yellow curling hair brushed his shoulder as she moved closer to him. She had the breasts of a goddess, perfect and heavy in his hands, with nipples that begged for the kind of attention that only he could give.

Heaven, Jess thought, pushing the sheet out of his way. He had died and gone to heaven and he was making love to...he didn't know her name. Ah, he sighed, nameless sex. Even better, even more mysterious. She shivered when his fingers swept up her thighs to that intimate place where he would soon join his body with hers...

She shifted, moved closer. She opened her eyes—light blue eyes the color of the sky in the morning—and smiled at him, and he fitted himself into her and—

Didn't use a condom? Jess opened his eyes and gasped for air. The motel room was too cold, the air-conditioning humming so loud that, for a moment, Jess didn't know where he was. Certainly not in bed making love to Lorna Walters.

He blinked and willed his memory to focus on that night. He'd had way too much to drink. He'd passed out—in her bed? He woke in the middle of the night and took a shower; he remembered a pink bathroom, a pink towel, perfumed soap. And then...he remembered making love to the woman in the bed.

The next thing he knew it was dawn. *Think, Sheridan. Think about condoms. Think about condom wrappers on the floor.*

He remembered nothing on the floor but a bath towel, his clothes and his cowboy boots. He had made love to Lorna six months ago without using protection? Had he been that stupid?

Jess switched on the light and swung his legs to the floor. He reached for his cell phone and punched in Chelsea's home phone number. The woman answered in seven rings.

"Chelsea. It's Sheridan."

"Okay," she said. "What's going on?"

"You knew Lorna Walters was pregnant."

"How could you miss it?" She yawned. "Is she okay? I mean, is this an emergency?"

"How pregnant?"

"Huh?"

Jess didn't have the patience to explain the facts to his secretary. "You know everything that goes on in town and you knew she was pregnant. That's why you looked at me funny when I told you I had a date with her."

"Let me think. Take a deep breath or something." He heard her fumbling with something. "Do you know it's four o'clock?"

"Chelsea—"

"Let's see," she drawled. "I'd better get emergency pay for this."

"I'll take you to lunch."

"She's due the same time as my cousin. I remember that much, because we were talking about it at the café and she said the date and I said, 'oh, that's the same time as my cousin' and she said she was due the fourth and my cousin is due the third and—"

His patience snapped. "What *month*?"

Chelsea sighed. "April. Because we were talking

about my grandmother, who was born on April Fool's Day and—"

"Thanks." He hung up. Lorna was due April fourth, so there must be a way to find out when she conceived. He called the Marysville hospital and asked to speak to a nurse in obstetrics.

"This is Sheriff Sheridan in Beauville." He used his most authoritative voice. "Quick question. If a woman is due April fourth, what was the day she conceived?"

"This is *who?*"

"Sheriff Jester S. Sheridan in Beauville, ma'am. I'd be real grateful for your assistance." He waited, hoping like hell that the nurse would take pity on him or at least believe that this was an official call.

"Just a minute, Sheriff. I might have one of those charts around here in a drawer somewhere."

He waited for what felt like an eternity. When the answer came, Jess dropped the phone on his big toe.

"IT'S MY BABY."

Lorna wished she hadn't opened the door. Jess didn't look happy. In fact, he looked downright terrible. He wore the same plaid shirt and khaki slacks from the night before, only the shirt was only half-buttoned, the slacks wrinkled and his usually neat hair was mussed, as if he had run his fingers through it a hundred times.

"It's *my* baby," he repeated, his dark eyes intent upon her face. "Isn't it?"

"Of course," Lorna said and stepped back to let him enter the house.

Jess looked surprised as he stared down at her. His hands held her shoulders. "It's my baby?"

"Yes." She stepped back and he released her.

"And you weren't going to tell me?"

"I was," she insisted, trying to wrap her robe around her midsection. It was times like this when she really missed her waist.

"When?"

"I thought you'd know." She noticed that he glanced at her abdomen and winced. That certainly wasn't very fatherly. "When you saw I was pregnant," she added. "I thought when you saw me you'd assume—"

"Assume I was going to be a father? Assume that one night in July when I was drunk I got someone pregnant?"

"It was a little bit of a surprise to me, too," Lorna told him, crossing her arms over her chest. "I have to get ready for work, so—"

"So we...had sex and didn't use any protection. That wasn't real smart, Lorna."

"There were two of us in the bed," she pointed out. "I've never bought a condom in my life, and before you I had sex twice. *Twice.* It was in college and my boyfriend supplied the, uh, protection."

A guilty expression swept over his handsome face. "I should have known better, I know. I hadn't, uh, been with anyone since my wife left."

So they were two inexperienced single people about to have a child. Lorna took pity on him. At least she'd had six months to get used to the idea. "Would you like some coffee?"

He gave her a blank look, so she repeated the offer.

"No," he said. "I came here to find out if I was going to be a father, not to have breakfast."

"Well, you found out. Now I have to go to work."

"And then what?"

"What do you mean?"

"After you have the baby, you can't work and take care of a baby."

"I have some money saved. And I own this house. I'll figure it out."

"We'll get married." He didn't look happy about it. "I'm not crazy about the idea, but there's no choice. The baby is going to need a father. And I'm willing to do my duty to you and the child."

"Do your duty?"

"Yes." He straightened to his full height, every

inch the protective male. "We don't know each other very well, but we're going to be parents. I think that calls for sacrifice."

"Sacrifice?"

"Besides," he said, obviously warming to the subject, "I don't want everyone in town knowing our business. We can say we've been secretly married since last summer."

"No one will believe that for a minute. And I don't—"

"Then we'll get married as soon as we can get a license." His frowned deepened. "We can drive to Dallas and do it so we don't have everyone around here gawking at us."

"I don't want to marry you." Not under these conditions, she didn't.

"I don't want to marry you either. You think I'm happy about this?" He threw his hands out, as if to emphasize his frustration. Lorna turned and headed toward the kitchen. "Where are you going?"

"You may not need coffee, but I do," she said, needing a break from the conversation more than she needed caffeine. He followed her into the small kitchen. She could feel his eyes on her as she retrieved a mug from the cupboard and filled it. "How did you figure all of this out, Sheriff?"

"I asked my secretary if she knew when you were due."

"Ah. The infamous Chelsea." She stopped every morning for a blueberry muffin and a cup of coffee, cream no sugar.

And she always had plenty to talk about. "So you counted backward."

"I checked with a nurse," he said. He leaned against the doorjamb and crossed his arms over his chest. "It was easy enough to figure out."

Lorna sat down at the small corner table, but she didn't ask Jess to join her. She took a sip of her coffee and looked at the clock above the refrigerator. She was going to be late for the first time in five and a half months, but Charlie would forgive her. He'd worry, though, so if she didn't get in to the café soon she knew he'd be calling her. "You could have asked me while we were having dinner."

"The thought that it was mine never crossed my mind." Her eyebrows rose at that statement, but she let him continue without interruption. "Nevertheless, we have a problem here. The sooner we face it the better."

"You can face anything you want," she said, sipping her coffee as if she didn't have a care in the world. "But I'm not going to marry you just to help you fulfill some sense of duty."

He gave her a blank look. "You don't have a choice. My son is not going to be born a bastard."

"My *daughter* is not going to grow up with parents who don't love each other and who only got married to save the sheriff some embarrassment."

"Daughter? Did the doctor tell you that?"

"Out," Lorna said, pointing her finger toward the front of the house. "Get out."

He didn't argue with her, although he opened his mouth and then closed it, as if he'd realized he'd said enough for one morning.

"Duty," she muttered, hurrying into the shower. Whatever happened to her dreams of happily ever after?

6

"YOU OWE ME a lunch," his secretary reminded Jess.

"Why?" Jimmy Carter, the overeager deputy, looked up from his computer. "What's going on?"

"Never mind," Jess told him. He tried to concentrate on his paperwork. There was always paperwork, especially since there seemed to be more and more regulations every year.

Chelsea grinned. "It's private."

"Nothing's private in this town," the younger man grumbled.

"You're just cranky 'cuz Bobby's dating both the Wynette twins again." Chelsea poured Jess a fresh cup of coffee and placed it on his desk. "You two have the worst luck of any men I've seen."

"Don't get me involved in this conversation," Jess warned. He had enough trouble trying to do his work while thinking of Lorna down the street at the Coffee Pot, just a few blocks away. He didn't intend to embarrass himself by going over there. Unless he got real hungry for lunch. Jess looked at the clock. Ten-thirty was too early for a burger and fries and a glimpse at his future wife.

"It's not fair," Carter said. "Calhoun gets all the women in town. A fine upstanding man like myself can't get diddly-squat when it comes to female attention." He looked over at his boss. "I heard you were out with the waitress at the café last night. Is Bobby Calhoun goin' out with her, too?"

"No." Jess looked at the phone and wished it would ring. A bank robbery right now would certainly take his mind off impending fatherhood. He'd never been so frightened in his entire life than he'd been since he found out he was going to be a daddy. What if it was a girl? Girls were delicate creatures and had feelings and cried a lot. He hoped for a boy. At least with a boy he could teach him guy stuff. And talk about football.

"Lorna's real pretty," the young man continued. "How old do you think she is?"

"Too old for you," Chelsea said. "And she's pregnant."

"I didn't say I was interested. I just wondered how old she was." He punched some buttons on the keyboard. "Darn thing's frozen again."

"Let me see." Chelsea hurried over to his side and leaned over his shoulder. Carter was too busy staring at the monitor to realize that the secretary was enjoying her close proximity to Carter, but Jess didn't miss it. "Here. Let's start over and I'll see what I can save."

"He gets all the women." The deputy moved out of

the way and turned to Jess, whose desk was only six feet away. "Don't let him get his hands on the waitress, boss. She'll never be the same."

"Bobby Calhoun is not dating Lorna." He didn't realize he was gritting his teeth until his jaws began to ache. "*I* am the only one dating her. In fact," he declared, only half realizing he was thinking out loud, "I'm going to marry her."

Two pairs of eyes stared at him. Carter's mouth dropped open and Chelsea's eyebrows rose.

"That was quick," she said. "After one date?"

"We've known each other a while."

"Six months?" His secretary ignored his stern look and grinned. "How's that for a brilliant guess?"

"We were neighbors when we were kids." He didn't want the word to get out that he and Lorna didn't really know each other. When the residents of Beauville discovered he'd married the café's pregnant waitress, he didn't want any gossip behind Lorna's back. He'd let people assume they'd been together for a while now, only waiting to get married until he'd returned from his job in Huntsville. No one need ever know the truth.

"Geez," Carter breathed. "You're gonna be a *father?*"

"Yeah. Why is that so hard to believe?" Jess wished he'd had breakfast. All of a sudden the coffee wasn't settling too well.

Carter didn't answer, but Chelsea picked up her appointment book. "So, when's the wedding, boss?"

"We're still discussing that."

"You shouldn't wait too long," Carter said. "She looks like she's gonna have that kid any day now."

"April fourth," Jess informed him. "That gives us almost three months. Plenty of time." And, he thought, turning away from their curious stares, he was going to need every day of those months to convince Lorna that getting married was the best thing for the baby. Couldn't she see that they didn't have any other choice?

LORNA'S DATE with the handsome new sheriff was the only topic of conversation during the breakfast rush.

"No wonder you were so nervous yesterday," Charlie said, setting out her order for table seven. "You were getting ready for your big date."

"It wasn't a big date."

Mike Monterro, sitting on his usual corner stool at the counter, sipped his lukewarm coffee and offered his own opinion. "Kinda strange, you going out on dates in your condition, but I guess it's about time you found a husband."

"I'm not getting married, Mike," Lorna said, and hurried away to deliver eggs, French toast and bacon to her waiting customers.

"She will," she heard Mike tell Charlie. "A child's got to have a father. Ain't right otherwise."

"Our new sheriff is a good-looking guy," the cook said. "Maybe he'll talk our Lorna into settling down."

"Whatever happened to his ex-wife?" someone asked, but Lorna didn't hear the reply. She prayed for patience. She wished her back would stop aching. She wanted to lie down and pretend that she was independently wealthy and could afford to lounge on a king-size bed while a maid brought her tea and sugar cookies. "Here you go," she told the four cowboys as she placed their meals in front of them. "Can I get you anything else?"

"More coffee?" one of them asked.

"Sure. I'll be right back with the pot." She waved at Emily, who slid into a booth with her youngest daughter beside her. "Hi. What are you doing out this morning?"

"We're going to story hour at the library at eleven," Emily explained. "We thought we'd have pancakes here first. Do you have a minute to tell me how your date went?"

"Just a sec." She grabbed the carafe, refilled the cowboys' coffee mugs and then fixed a mug for Emily. Lorna looked over toward the serving counter and saw that it was empty, so she sat down across from her friend. "For a minute," she said. "It's pretty busy this morning."

"The sheriff brought you roses. I saw him run out to his rig and get them. Why didn't you tell me you were going out with Jess Sheridan?"

"You know him?"

"He lived outside of town when he was a deputy, Lorna. Everyone knows him. So, how was the date?"

Lorna sighed. It felt so darn good to sit down for a minute. "It had its ups and downs."

"He noticed the pregnancy, of course."

"And he never said a word." Not until dawn. And then the words he'd spoken were not the ones she'd wanted to hear. *I'm willing to do my duty to you and the child.*

"That's amazing."

"You don't know the half of it."

"Lorna! Order's up!"

She glanced over at the counter. "I've got to go. I'll take your order first." She smiled at Elly. "Blueberry pancakes and chocolate milk?"

"Yes, please." The toddler grinned up at her. "I love pancakes."

"And I'll have blueberry pancakes, too. Without the chocolate milk," Emily said. "Join us again if you have a second, okay? I want to hear everything."

And so did everyone else in the café that morning, Lorna thought later on, in the lull before the lunch rush began. She hadn't had time to talk to Emily again, except to tell her she'd call when she got home from work. The lunch crowd kept her busy. Somehow two of her regular lunch customers knew about the roses. Someone else had seen her with the sheriff at the Steak Barn. Almost everyone wanted to know what was going on, but Lorna just smiled and said things like, "We're old friends," and "I had a real nice time."

She couldn't believe it was of that much interest to so many people. Even Chelsea, the interesting-looking secretary from Jess's office, winked at her when she came in to pick up the office order.

"He's cranky today," the girl whispered. "What'd you do to him?"

"Not a darn thing," Lorna replied, handing her a large brown paper bag filled with sandwiches, potato chips and dessert. She punched the numbers on the cash register and took the money Chelsea handed her.

Charlie waved to Chelsea. Lorna knew they were related somehow, but she'd never understood the complicated connection. "Did you hear Lorna had a date?" he called.

"I sure did." Chelsea leaned across the counter and lowered her voice so that only Lorna could hear. "He called me at four this morning to ask me when your baby was due. So I guess you two have known each other a long time, huh?"

"That's right." The doorbell jangled and, out of

habit, Lorna glanced toward the door. Jess entered, his gaze directly on her as he approached the counter where she stood behind the cash register.

"Hi, honey," he said, loud enough for anyone within ten feet to hear. And he smiled, but he didn't look as if he really meant it.

"Hi, Sheriff," Lorna managed, and gave Chelsea her change.

"She called him 'sheriff,'" someone said. "Ain't that cute."

Chelsea winked at her and moved out of her boss's way. "I ordered your lunch," she told him, lifting the bag.

"Save it for me 'til later, will you?" he said. "I'll be back at the office in a while." Then Jess turned to Lorna. "I'm taking a ride out to a ranch south of here. Want to go with me?"

"I can't," she said, glad for the excuse. "I'm working."

"When do you get off?"

"Two o'clock," she said, conscious of the customers listening to every word. She assumed that was why Jess was inviting her in front of practically everyone in town.

"Good," he said. "I'll pick you up then."

"I didn't say yes," she whispered, ignoring Charlie's call that her order was ready. "And I'm really busy here."

"Can I get a cup of coffee, then?" He slid onto the only empty stool at the counter.

She poured him coffee and set the mug in front of him without saying anything.

"Lorna, hon, where do you want to have dinner tonight?"

"I'm busy." She turned away to retrieve Mr. Monterro's hamburger and fries from the counter and gave it to him, along with a ketchup bottle. Mr. Monterro liked his ketchup.

"You got a date with someone *else* tonight?" The elderly man looked shocked. "Missy, you'd better settle down before that baby comes."

"I didn't say I had a date." Lorna turned to Jess. He looked a lot better than he had at five this morning. Now he looked very much like the self-controlled professional, with a neatly pressed tan button-down shirt tucked into khaki pants and a badge on his shirt pocket. "What are you doing here?"

"Having coffee," he said. "Seeing you. Checking on the baby."

"The baby is fine," she told him, conscious of Mr. Monterro listening to every word. The man on the other side of Jess, a grizzled rancher, winked at her.

"Are you sure you don't want to take a ride this afternoon? Get some fresh air? We could stop in and see the Johnsons on the way back, then get something to eat." He gave her an innocent smile, but she wasn't fooled. He was up to something, coming in here and calling her "honey" in front of everyone like that.

"I have a doctor's appointment at two-thirty." There. That would scare him off.

He frowned. "Something serious?"

"No. My monthly checkup."

"I see." He looked thoughtful. "Is that an invitation?"

"No." She didn't want him pretending to be interested, pretending to want to be a father. He would see it as just another duty that he needed to fulfill.

"Then what?"

"Then I go home and put on an aerobics video."

Mike leaned closer. "What's that?"

"A bad joke," she sighed, picking up a cloth to wipe the counter. Jess finished his coffee and she didn't offer to refill it. He stayed at the counter while she delivered food to the tables and booths; it was a busy time of day and would continue like that for another hour or so. Lorna didn't mind. The sheriff would soon have to go arrest someone or whatever it was he did in a sleepy town like Beauville.

Sure enough, after she returned from delivering seven more lunches, Jess was gone. He'd left a couple of dollars under his empty cup. She told herself she was glad he'd gone on his way. Maybe he'd accepted her refusal to marry him, but somehow Lorna knew he wouldn't give up that easily.

If only he could give her what she really wanted. A chance at love.

"A MAN'S GOTTA DO what a man's gotta do," Jess muttered, facing the building. It was just a building, after all. Two-storied brick on West Cotton Street, it shouldn't have looked particularly intimidating, but Jess hesitated before climbing the cement steps to the double doors, the entrance to Beauville's medical building. Next door was a new walk-in clinic, but the town's medical building housed a laboratory, chiropractor, dentists, and assorted physicians. The obstetrician came to town on Wednesdays and Saturdays to see her pregnant patients outside of Marysville, a long hour's drive northeast of town.

Jess didn't have Saturday nights off usually, but he'd arranged with Carter to take over at ten, which gave the younger man a chance to go out looking for women or something equally exciting to a twenty-four-year-old bachelor. And gave Jess the chance to spend the rest of the day with Lorna. It was going to take some time to convince her that they should get married, for the baby's sake, but she would come around eventually.

And he hoped soon. Before there was any more talk.

So Jess found the right office, strode into the waiting room and prepared to do battle with Lorna for the right to accompany her to see the doctor. Several pregnant women stared when he walked in. He went up to the desk and tapped on the Plexiglas window.

"Yes? Can I help you?" The gray-haired receptionist slid the window open.

"Yes, ma'am. Lorna Walters had a two-thirty appointment. Is she with the doctor?"

"Are you an expectant father or are you here in an official capacity?"

"Expectant father," he whispered.

Her eyebrows rose as if she didn't believe a word he said. "We haven't seen you in here before."

"Well, I'm here now and I'd like to talk to the doctor and see my—" Jess stopped, unsure what to call Lorna. "Girlfriend" was juvenile, "wife" was a little premature. "Fiancée," he said, trying out the word. That worked for him and must have worked for the receptionist, because she pointed to a side door.

"Go in there and the nurse will take you to her."

"Thanks." He went through the door, recognized the young nurse as someone who used to live with her parents on a ranch near him and Sue, and was led to a closed door. The nurse knocked and then ushered Jess into the examining room, where Lorna lay on a table with her belly exposed.

He gulped, then met her gaze. "Sorry I'm late, honey." He turned to the doctor, a thirtyish woman with a dark-haired braid down her back and brown eyes that didn't look as if they missed a thing. "I'm Jess Sheridan, the new sheriff and the, uh, future father."

"The father?" Dr. Bradford glanced toward Lorna, who didn't contradict his statement. She turned back to Jess. "Nice to meet you, Sheriff. I was just telling Lorna that she needs to get more rest. Her blood pressure was a little high, which is something we're going to keep an eye on."

Jess looked at Lorna, who didn't look too upset that he was there, which was a good sign. "Are you okay?"

"I'm fine," she assured him.

The doctor picked up something that looked like a microphone. "We were just about to see how your baby is doing. Watch the monitor and you'll see."

"IS HE GOING TO BE OKAY?"

"He'll be fine," the nurse insisted. "Let him sit here until he isn't dizzy anymore and then have him stand slowly. Take your time and don't try to leave until you're ready," she said, and left them alone in the examining room.

Lorna perched on the doctor's metal stool and eyed Jess. He was unusually pale. She hadn't seen him horizontal since July. "Are you always this pathetic?"

"I never used to think so," he muttered, eyes closed. He lay stretched out on the table, pillows under his knees to elevate his legs so that the blood would rush back to his head. "It only happens when I'm around you."

"It was just an ultrasound," she said, trying not to laugh. "It doesn't hurt me or the baby."

"I know that. Now."

"What are you doing here? Besides passing out, I mean." She tried not to like him, she really did. A childhood crush and a one-night stand didn't qualify to really know the man, but she liked him. Had even loved him, or thought she did when she was a silly teenager. And now? Now she wished they could start over, as two adults with no past to complicate things.

"I'm the father. I thought I should show support."

Another *should*. "Your duty," she said.

"Yeah." He opened his eyes and turned his head toward her. "You *are* going to marry me, you know."

"I can't."

"You have to."

"But you don't love me," she said, and hoped she didn't sound wistful. "A marriage should begin with love and commitment and—"

"Love doesn't have anything to do with it. I thought I loved my first wife," he said, struggling to sit up. "Look how that ended."

"How?"

"She ran off with another man. Said it was love at first sight and she couldn't—wouldn't—live without him." He ran his fingers through his hair and slid off the table to stand on his booted feet. "It was the most ridiculous thing I ever heard in my life."

And, Lorna guessed, the most painful. "You must have loved her very much." He gave her an odd look and shook his head, then tilted sideways. "Are you okay?" She stood to grab his elbow. His shirt felt warm under her fingers, the muscles above his elbow hard to the touch.

"Yeah." He plucked his Stetson off the counter lined with medical supplies and settled it on his head. "I'll be better next month," he promised. "At least I'll know what's coming up on the TV screen."

"If you saw that it was a boy, don't tell me," she said.

"Honey, I saw a baby in there. I sure as hell didn't get a chance to recognize any, uh, special equipment before the room started spinning."

"Good. I want to be surprised."

"Honey, you're going to kill me if there are any-more surprises." He took her hand and opened the door. "In the last twenty-four hours, I've had all I can handle."

"You just need some time to adjust," she assured him. "And you know you're welcome to be part of the baby's life in whatever way you want."

He stopped short of leaving the room and glared down at her. "I hate to keep repeating myself, honey, but we're getting married. Just what about that isn't clear to you?"

"I'm not going to marry someone who has to marry me because I'm pregnant."

The nurse walked past and smiled at them. "Are you feeling better, Sheriff?"

"Yes, ma'am. Believe it or not, I do better at crime scenes than with pregnancy."

"Typical male," the nurse declared. "Now that you're on your feet, take Lorna home and put her to bed."

"Yes, ma'am, that's exactly what I want to do." He tugged on Lorna's hand and led her down the hall. Lorna didn't argue. Given a choice between riding out to some ranch with Jess or curling up in her bed, she'd pick the bed this afternoon.

It was too bad Jess wasn't going to be in it with her.

ered with a multicolored quilt. At least the pillows
weren't piled against the carved and detailed headboard
of the bed. An invalid's bed, Jess wouldn't have
minded sinking down in it either. The door at the
back...

7

"GO TO BED, LORNA," he said, following her into her
house. "Now."

"Do I look like I'm going to argue with you?" Actually Lorna didn't look like she was going to argue
with him at all. Jess just liked telling her to get into
bed.

Not that he was thinking about sex. He needed to
redeem himself after the disgraceful fainting incident
in the doctor's office. If it ever got out that he'd let a
little thing like an ultrasound make him weak in the
knees, he'd be laughed out of the county.

"Not really. I just like bossing you around."

"You can stop anytime." She even yawned, to
prove her point or maybe because she was sleepy,
Jess didn't know. "Don't you have to go be a sheriff?"

"Not until ten o'clock, or unless Carter needs me."
He followed her into the bedroom. It looked different, though the bed was in the same place, to the right
of the door and across from a set of windows. The
white walls looked freshly painted, there was a bright
braided rug on the wood floor, and the bed was cov-

ered with a multicolored quilt. At least six pillows were piled against the curving metal headboard, giving the bed an inviting look. Jess wouldn't have minded sinking down into it either. The door at the opposite end, he knew, led to the hall and the bathroom.

"You don't have to stay," Lorna said. She sat on the edge of the bed and managed to untie her shoelaces before Jess realized that her pregnancy made the chore awkward. "I'm perfectly capable of taking care of myself."

"Yeah," he said. "But you don't have to. The nurse told me to take you home and make sure you got some rest so that's what I'm going to do."

"How did you get in the examining room, anyway?" She eased herself off the bed and headed toward the bathroom.

"I told the receptionist I was your fiancé," he said, as she shut the door and left him alone in the room. It was immaculately clean, with photos on the surface of the oak dresser and a gilded mirror hanging above it.

She muttered something he couldn't understand, and then a few moments later came out of the bathroom dressed in a flowered cotton nightgown that showed absolutely nothing of her body but turned him on more than he'd ever been in his life. He didn't know why, except that this woman affected him that way. "Goodbye, Jess." Lorna went directly to the bed and pulled the quilt back to expose pale yellow sheets and climbed into the bed. She leaned back against the pillows and sighed with contentment.

"I can fix you something to eat." She did look pale and he hadn't noticed those dark smudges under her eyes until now when the sunlight came through the windows and highlighted her face.

"I'm not hungry." She scooted down under the covers and, almost as an afterthought, smiled at him. "Go away, Jess."

"Okay," he agreed. "I'll leave my number so you can page me whenever you need me."

"I won't need you," Lorna said, but her voice was soft and she didn't seem upset with him anymore. He didn't know what possessed him, but in three strides he was at the side of the bed. Jess bent down and touched his lips to hers. He meant it to be brief, just the barest of kisses to show her that he was in her life now. It was to have been a "sleep well" kind of kiss, but Lorna's lips were so very soft and she leaned toward him just a little, enough to guarantee she wasn't going to belt him when the kiss was over.

So he took his time. He braced himself by holding on to the headboard with one hand, the other held Lorna's chin and kept her mouth against his. He slanted his mouth, deepened the kiss, swept his tongue across her parted lips and, reluctantly, fought the immediate passion that made him think of crawling into bed with her and making love for the rest of the afternoon. It was almost painful to move his fingers away from her face, to withdraw his kiss and move away from the bed.

"I'll drive by periodically," he promised. "I won't stop unless I see your bedroom light on and know you're awake."

She closed her eyes and turned away from him to snuggle into the nest of pillows, so Jess left the room and headed for the front door. There would be no trip out to the ranch to see how the old place was holding up. He would stay close, in case Lorna paged him.

He didn't regret kissing her. He might even think about it a few times this afternoon as he went about his business. When he was around her he wanted her. Simple as that.

But part of him knew there was nothing simple about it.

"IT'S HIS BABY," Chelsea declared. "I'll bet anything that it is."

"Uh, I don't know." Carter didn't look convinced. "Sheridan's always been a pretty straight arrow. I can't picture him getting someone pregnant."

"I don't want to picture it either, believe me, but from the way he's acting I'm sure this is his baby. How do you think he knows Lorna? He said they were old friends, but I don't believe that for a minute."

"Why not?"

"Something isn't right about that story," she mused, eyeing the deputy as he typed—two-fingered—at the computer. She really should have pursued a career as a police detective instead of going to business school. She was so much smarter than Carter, though he was the handsomest thing in Beauville. In the brains department there was something missing, but she liked him anyway. Too bad he was obsessed with the Wynette twins who, in Chelsea's opinion, needed to get off the ranch and get their hair and nails done.

"Well, he says he's getting married," Carter conceded. "I guess he wouldn't be marrying her if it wasn't his baby."

"Lorna conceived July 12."

"How'd you know that?"

"I found a Web site. What was going on around here then? Was Jess in Huntsville?" Carter shrugged. Honestly, she didn't know how he ever passed the deputy sheriff exam.

"Rings a bell," he said, frowning off into space while Chelsea dug out last year's schedule. Her predecessor had been as meticulous a record-keeper as Chelsea herself.

"Got it," she said, finding July. "July twelfth was Jake Johnson's wedding."

"Guess Jess felt romantic."

"I think all weddings are romantic," Chelsea mused, picturing herself wearing a flowing lacy gown and a veil made of sparkly silver net to match her hair. She would have silver fingernails and a platinum wedding band and a diamond that would outshine the sun.

"Not me," the handsome deputy said. He glanced at the clock and pushed back his desk chair. "Guess it's time for me to make rounds."

"We need to do something."

"About what?" He strapped on his gun and grabbed his hat.

"The wedding. What if we gave them a bridal shower?"

"I don't think Jess would like that."

"It would be a surprise. He wouldn't have to know anything about it until it happened." The poor man looked even more confused than usual, so Chelsea added, "That's what usually happens, you know. The showers are a surprise. That's the fun part, along with the presents."

"Oh." He shrugged. "I guess you know more about that stuff than me."

Duh. "Then you agree with me."

"Yeah." Carter edged toward the door. Chelsea figured all this wedding talk was making him nervous.

"I'll keep you posted," she called after him, then looked at the phone. She loved this part of her job.

LORNA SURVEYED HER KITCHEN COUNTER. Piles of food had been left there while she napped and, when she opened the refrigerator, she saw stacks of cheese, quarts of milk and assorted fruits and vegetables. She wanted love and romance and instead she got one kiss and a couple of hundred dollars' worth of groceries. Jess had an odd idea of how to please a woman.

She opened a bag of chocolate chip cookies, the kind that advertised "extra chips," and bit into one. Maybe Jess hadn't been completely off track after all. It was almost seven o'clock; she'd slept for more than three hours. The baby's somersaults had wakened her, along with hunger and a cramp in her lower back. And, she admitted, a desire to see if Jess was anywhere around.

She checked the messages on her machine: Emily wanted to hear more about her date last night, Charlie requested that she could work a dinner shift instead of her usual breakfast and lunch next Thursday night and Jess asked her to call him when she woke up. He also reminded her of his number, which she dialed.

"Sheridan," came the official response after one ring.

"Jess? It's Lorna."

"How are you?"

"I'm fine. Really."

"Good. I'll be right over." The line disconnected, leaving Lorna holding the receiver in one hand and the bag of cookies in the other.

She tossed the cookies on the table and hurried to get dressed. If she wasn't going to marry him, she shouldn't be prancing around in her nightgown, modest as it was. And she shouldn't let him into her bedroom again, although she'd wanted to pull him into bed with her and snuggle into his arms and maybe even more. According to the pregnancy book she'd bought, having sex was permissible into the ninth month unless your doctor said otherwise.

Lorna didn't think Jess was interested in having sex with her. It most likely didn't fit into his idea of "duty," at least not now. How depressing. And yet, there were times when she felt about as glamorous as a kangaroo. And other times, when Jess looked at her a certain way, that she wanted to dissolve into a puddle of passion. Lorna looked at herself in the mirror after putting on elastic waist maternity jeans and a white T-shirt the size of a Titanic life raft. She really needed to get a grip. Maybe she could blame this whole thing with Jess on hormones. It was always easy to blame hormones, because no one understood them enough to have a conflicting opinion.

"It's hormones," she explained, when she opened the door and let the father of her child into her house.

"Okay," he said, as if she'd just said "nice day." "*What's* hormones?"

"The reason that sometimes I like to see you and have you around."

"Hurray for hormones." He handed her a very cold paper bag, and when she peered inside she saw a container of Ben & Jerry's Chunky Monkey ice cream.

"Don't get used to them," she warned. "They fluctuate at lightning speed. And thanks for dessert. How did you know?"

"Chelsea. My secretary is a fountain of female information."

Lorna headed for the kitchen and hoped she wasn't waddling. She didn't think she was expected to waddle until the eighth month, but then again—

"I told her and Carter, my deputy, that we were getting married."

Lorna shoved the ice cream in the freezer compartment and turned around. "Why did you do an awful thing like that?"

He smiled and put his hands on her shoulders. They were large and warm and strangely comforting.

"Because you're having my baby and my son is not going to grow up without a father."

"And what if it's a girl?"

"Girls need fathers, too."

"Look," she said, wishing she didn't like him so much. She'd always been a little bit in love with him, too, which didn't make it easy to refuse a convenient alternative to single motherhood. "I've given this some thought. You'll have unlimited access to the baby. I want him or her to have a father in his or her life. I won't prevent that, Jess. I think it's important."

"Are you talking about joint custody, moving the child from my house to yours all the time?"

Speechless, she shook her head. Her child wasn't going to live with anyone else but her mother. "Of course not. What happens when you get married?"

"Or when you do?" he countered. "See how complicated this gets if you think about the future?"

Lorna's eyes filled up with tears and Jess didn't help by putting his arms around her and cradling her against his very wide chest. Her belly bumped his belt, but he didn't seem to mind.

"Marry me, Lorna," he said, his voice rumbling against her ear. "We have to do the right thing for the child. We'll give him a home and security and health insurance—the county employees have a pretty decent health plan—and you won't have to wait tables until your feet hurt."

"You're so practical," she sniffled. "And you don't love me."

"It's not exactly in the picture right now, honey."

"Because of your wife?"

"Ex-wife," he growled, resting his chin on top of her head. "To be real honest with you, Lorna, I'm not sure I even know what being in love is all about."

Lorna sighed against his chest. "You brought me ice cream," she said. "I guess that's a pretty good start."

"Does that mean you agree to the plan?"

She so wished he wouldn't refer to their marriage as "the plan." "It means I'm thinking."

"Take your time," the man said. "But I'd prefer to get this whole thing over with."

IT SEEMED AS THOUGH everyone in Beauville knew there was going to be a wedding between their new sheriff and the pregnant waitress. Oh, Jess Sheridan had been around town for ten years or so, since his days as a young deputy. He was well respected for his ability to be fair and even-tempered, even under difficult circumstances, so no one was really surprised that he would step up and marry the woman they assumed he'd made pregnant.

And she seemed like a nice enough woman, always a smile in the morning and ready with the coffeepot when a customer needed a refill. Charlie, a heck of a good cook even if he did give as many opinions as he sold burgers, spoke highly of the little blond waitress. There were some folk who thought they remembered her as a child in Marysville, others wondered if they might have gone to high school with her—Beauville teens were bussed to the large high school in that neighboring town. Gert Knepper, the oldest woman in town, declared that Lorna's folks had been those square-dancing people who used to do a show at the county fair each fall. And Gert also remembered that Lorna's aunt—the woman who painted her house pink before she got too old to lift a paintbrush—had sure kept a nice garden.

Her daughter Martha agreed and said that Emily Bennett, who went to school with Martha's famous New York City daughter, told her that she'd never had a nicer neighbor than Lorna Walters.

Chelsea talked of organizing the wedding reception and waited for her boss to write the date of his wedding in his appointment book. Emily Bennett whispered of a baby shower, women only, thank you. Charlie swore he saw the sheriff talking to Joey at his jewelry store, but so far none of the customers at the Coffee Pot had seen a diamond ring on the third finger of Lorna's left hand when she put their checks on the counter.

No one dared talk to Bobby Calhoun about weddings; he was still sensitive about the cancellation of his own, even if it had been six months since his heart broke over that girl in Paris, France. Bobby recently got into trouble again when some young idiot bet him he couldn't ride two horses at once down Main Street. Someone said that Jess had spent all last weekend trying to get the kid to sober up and get control of himself, so maybe he hadn't had time to buy a ring after all.

So the residents of Beauville—most of them, anyway—were willing to overlook the fact that the sheriff and the waitress had gotten a little ahead of themselves and made the baby before they made the vows. When whispers of a wedding began, helped along by Chelsea Higgs, who should know, folks looked forward to helping the young folks celebrate. Sheridan had gotten a raw deal the first time around, his friends said. Maybe this time would be better. It sure couldn't be any worse.

Jess Sheridan would have agreed with them. At the bookstore in Marysville, he bought two books about child care and one about pregnancy written especially for the fathers-to-be. He'd given Lorna a few days to think things over; it was now time to figure out the rest of their lives. Which was exactly what he told her answering machine Wednesday evening.

By Thursday morning he'd run out of patience. The breakfast crowd at the Coffee Pot was at its height, meaning Jess had to stand next to Mike Monterro and wait for a stool. He didn't see Lorna anywhere, and the waitress who appeared from the back of the restaurant was someone he didn't recognize.

"Where's Lorna?" He tried to get Charlie's attention by waving, but the cook gave him a nod and kept right on frying eggs.

"Not here today," Mike said. "When's the wedding?"

"We haven't decided yet." The man next to Mike reached for his wallet, so with luck a spot would open up soon. "Why? Are folks that interested?"

"Oh, yeah, they sure are, Sheriff," the old man declared. "Not a lot going on around here these days, so I guess you're the prime topic of conversation. Folks are real curious as to how this all came about."

He winced, wondering if anyone besides he and Lorna knew he'd spent the night with her last summer. It would be one more juicy piece of gossip for those who liked to exchange rumors. The stool empty, Jess slid into place. The waitress brought him a cup of coffee, but he didn't order breakfast. "Where's Lorna?"

"We switched shifts," the girl explained. "She'll be on at four."

"Can I give you some advice?" the man asked, setting down his coffee cup and turning slightly so that he faced Jess.

"Sure." He braced himself, having heard diaper

jokes for the past three days. From the way parents talked, babies didn't do anything but poop, pee and puke for the first six months of their lives.

"You've got to stop draggin' your heels, son."

"She's the one taking her time, Mike," Jess admitted. "If you have any advice on how to talk her into getting married real soon, well, I'd sure like to hear it."

"Flowers," he said.

"Tried that. Yellow roses, in fact."

"Candy, then. My wife had a sweet tooth and I could always get her to forgive me if I handed over a box of chocolates."

Jess thought of the ice cream and chocolate chip cookies. "Yeah, I've done that, too. She seemed happy about it, but she wouldn't agree to marry me right away."

"Well," the old man drawled. "That's difficult. Gets more expensive."

"I'm not going to get down on my knees and beg," he said. "But I'm damn well not going to take no for an answer."

Mike sighed. "Heard a rumor you were over at Joe's looking at jewelry."

He shook his head. "I replaced the battery in my watch."

"Guess you'd better get back there then and go

shopping. Women expect an engagement ring, Sheriff."

Jess frowned. He took a sip of coffee and gave that some thought. Rings were expensive. Sue hadn't wanted any of the jewelry his grandmother had offered him, and he'd ended up financing a diamond ring that cost four months' salary. Looking back, he realized he should have protested. But he wanted to make her happy—or at least try. "Women expect a lot of things," Jess said. "Some of them are downright impossible to do."

"You talking about your ex-wife or your future one?" Mike cackled, figuring he'd made a pretty good joke.

"I guess I'd better go shopping," he told the old man. He left his unfinished coffee and headed across the street to the jewelry store. There was a knot in his stomach the size of the Hope Diamond before he even reached the first display case.

"WHAT DO YOU THINK?"

Emily eyed the brand-new crib, the simplest one of the seventeen displayed in the furniture store. "I like it, Lorna."

"Really?" She touched the white rails and pictured her baby asleep in her bed. "So do I. I think I'm going to get it. Do you think they deliver?"

"Save your money and have your sheriff pick it

up," her friend declared. "Where did Elizabeth go off to?"

"She went to look at rocking chairs," Lorna said. "She said she can't decide whether to get a new one or an antique."

"Uh-oh. I've been shopping with her before, when she was furnishing Jake's old ranch house. That means she's going to want to stop at every antique store in Marysville to check the prices." Emily chuckled. "I've never been pregnant with two other girlfriends before. This is fun."

Oh, it was definitely that, Lorna thought. When she'd discovered she would have Thursday free, she'd asked Emily's advice on baby furniture. One thing led to another after Emily ran into Elizabeth at the grocery store, and the three of them climbed into Emily's large Suburban and set out to shop 'til they dropped—or at least until after lunch, when they would have to get back so Lorna could go to work.

"Have you known Elizabeth long?"

"Not really," Emily said, waving over the salesman. "She married the cousin of my best friend from high school. From what Kate says, the whole family just loves her."

"She's very beautiful." Next to tall and elegant Mrs. Johnson, Lorna felt short, dumpy and tempted to cut her rambunctious curls.

"I think there's more to Elizabeth than we think,"

Emily whispered. "Anyone who would put her dog in a tuxedo and invite him to her wedding has to be pretty darn adventurous."

Lorna laughed. "You might be right, Em." She told the salesman she wanted the crib and gave him her credit card.

"You haven't seen her house, have you?"

"No." She'd been too tired to accept Jess's invitation to ride out there. She wondered if he would ask her again. "Not yet."

"You're going to love it. She takes really old furniture, the kind of stuff our mothers and grandmothers would have tossed out, and makes it look great."

Elizabeth stepped around a display of upholstery fabric and walked toward them. "You wouldn't believe how much a new rocking chair costs," she said, as she drew closer. "I like the old ones better."

"I just told Lorna about your house. And your dog. And how you're going to want to go to antique stores before we go home." Emily grinned. "Was I wrong?"

"No." Elizabeth smiled at both of them. "But lunch comes first—with dessert, because we're all eating for two now."

Lorna couldn't wait. "I like the way you think."

"Oh, we're going to have fun," Emily assured her. "I'm going to teach you two everything I know about babies."

The salesman returned with Lorna's bill. "Do you want it delivered, ma'am?"

"No," she said. "My—friend will pick it up." He gave her the information on where and when to get the crib, then gave her the receipt. "Thank you."

"Good luck, ma'am," he said. "Can I help anyone else?"

"I'll be back," Elizabeth promised. "I have more time than Lorna does."

"Let me give you your first piece of advice," Emily said. "Don't let the sheriff put the crib together by himself unless you're sure he's some kind of mechanical genius."

"I'm not sure he'll want to," she admitted. He hadn't spoken to her much in the past few days. Maybe he was giving her time to think about his proposal. Or maybe he'd changed his mind about the whole thing. "The last three times he's asked me to marry him I've said no."

"Three times?" Emily almost tripped over a velvet hassock, but Elizabeth caught her arm. "Don't you *want* to marry him?"

"Of course I do. But he doesn't love me."

Elizabeth sighed. "Oh, Lorna, I'm sorry. Sometimes these Texan men get strange ideas in their heads. Give it time. Maybe he cares for you more than you know."

"I don't think so. The first time he asked me he

talked about doing his duty. The last time he talked
about marriage, he said he wanted to 'get it over
with.'"

"Oh, Lorna," Emily moaned, but Lorna smiled and
her friend burst into laughter. "That's the *worst* proposal I ever heard."

"Oh, dear," Elizabeth said. "No wonder you said
no."

"You can get even with him, you know." The redhead smiled. "Ask him to put the crib together."

"Really?" It would also give her an excuse to call
him. To see him.

"Absolutely," Emily promised. "It's a project guar-
anteed to drive him crazy."

"Or you could give him another chance," Elizabeth
said. "These Texas men really are worth the wait."

8

HE'D CAUGHT ON that Lorna was nicer to him when she was tired. She needed him to tell her to sit down and rest, or go to bed, things like that. So Jess waited until right before nine, the time the Coffee Pot closed, before stepping inside the café. No doubt she'd need him a lot by the end of the evening shift.

"Hey, Sheriff." Charlie sat on a stool, a cup of steaming coffee in front of him. "Kitchen's closed, but I'll bet you didn't come for food."

"No, I—"

"Lorna!" the cook bellowed. "You've got company! Your boyfriend's here!"

Jess thought he was a little old to be referred to as someone's boyfriend. "I can come back if this is a bad—"

"Hi, Jess." Lorna stepped out of the kitchen. "What are you doing here?"

"Looking for you." She wore one of Charlie's grease-stained white aprons, which covered her from her breasts to her knees. Her face was flushed and her hair, caught up in a lopsided ponytail, frizzed around her face. There was a dark smudge on her cheek and her hands were covered with yellow rubber gloves. She looked as if she'd been cleaning for hours, a thought that made him want to pick her up and haul her out of there. Jess took a deep breath, but he knew he sounded angry when he asked, "What the *hell* are you doing, Lorna?"

"Cleaning the kitchen."

"She volunteered," Charlie hurried to add. "I told her to go home but she wouldn't hear of it."

"The boy that usually comes in to do the dishes is sick and Charlie's knee is bothering him again," Lorna explained, coming closer to him. "I'm almost done. Do you want to know what I bought today?"

"I want to know when you're taking off that apron," he snapped, angry at himself for feeling so protective. This fatherhood business was tough, especially when the future mother insisted upon working too hard.

Lorna merely smiled. "I went shopping in Marysville with Emily Bennett and Elizabeth Johnson today."

Shopping? When she should have been resting? Jess bit back his frustration and managed a terse, "Really."

"And I'm going to need your help."

That was more like it, Jess thought. "Sure. With what?"

"If you'll drive me home in about twenty minutes, I'll explain it to you."

"All right." He paused. "Wait a minute. You walked to work?"

"Most of the time that's exactly what I do," she said. "The doctor said that walking is good exercise."

"Cleaning kitchens isn't." He glared at Charlie. "You should know better."

"She's hard to argue with," the cook said, and slid off his stool. "Go home, Lorna. The sheriff's right."

"But I'm not done with—"

"Go," he insisted. "I'll finish up."

"You're a lot nicer than Texas Tom," she said, removing the apron and the gloves. She handed them to her boss.

"So are rattlesnakes," the cook said. "Take your sheriff out of here and go home."

"Thanks." She retrieved her purse from under the counter and emptied her tips into an envelope. "See you in the morning, Charlie."

Jess hustled her out the front door before she could change her mind. He tucked her into the front seat of the car and watched to make sure she fastened her seat belt. He'd read in the pregnancy book that it was essential that expectant mothers never neglected to use seat belts. With that done, he went around to the driver's side and got in.

"You're off duty?" she asked.

"Yeah. I took the day shift." He did a U-turn in the middle of the empty street and headed toward Lorna's house. "I looked for you this morning, but Charlie told me you'd be working tonight."

"I haven't seen much of you lately."

That surprised him. "I had coffee at the café every morning. What did you buy in Marysville?"

"The crib." Her smile almost made him run the curb, which wouldn't have made the folks at the newspaper building happy. "Would you help me put it together?"

"Sure. No problem." He would move mountains, catch the sun and divert the course of the Rio Grande if she would smile at him again.

"Thanks. Emily said it can be tricky."

"Honey, I can manage," he assured her. There would be directions. He carried a tool kit in the trunk. "I'll do it tonight."

"Oh, I don't have it yet. It's still in Marysville. I told them you would pick it up. If you can't," she hurried to add, "they deliver. I just thought—"

"You'd save the fifty-dollar delivery fee. Good idea." He pulled up in front of her yard and waited for an invitation to come inside. He didn't expect one, but he couldn't help hoping she'd come to her senses and realize how much she needed a man in her life. And not just any man, either.

"I can show you a picture of it." She rummaged

through her purse and pulled out a brochure. "It's the white one on the cover," she said, handing it to him. Jess switched on the inside light and examined a picture of a crib. It didn't look like anything special to him—a crib was a crib, wasn't it?—but the expression of joy on Lorna's face was worth pretending interest.

"Real nice," he said, trying to picture what his son or daughter would look like sleeping in that crib. No, he couldn't imagine having a baby. Not even after looking at those pictures in the books.

"Come on," she said, opening her door. "I'll show you the baby's room."

"Uh, okay." Cribs and nurseries were not exactly what he had in mind tonight, not with a bag of jewelry sitting in the glove compartment and another marriage proposal stuck in his throat. Still, an invitation was an invitation and he wasn't going to turn down a chance to be with her. She hopped out, not noticing that he leaned over and took something from the glove compartment and tucked it into his jacket pocket. Tonight was the night.

The baby's room was next to Lorna's, a corner room tucked in between Lorna's bedroom and the bathroom. He'd noticed the closed door before, but hadn't paid any attention to it.

"It's pink," he said, staring at the walls, the curtains, the rug and even the ceiling light fixture, a ceramic rose hanging upside down. "*Really* pink."

"Aunt Carol went through a pink phase when she was in her fifties. There are some rooms I haven't had time to paint yet." Lorna chuckled. "It's really awful, isn't it?"

"The kid will have nightmares."

"I'll get it done before she's born."

"You shouldn't be on a ladder," he muttered. "Do you have paint?"

"Gallons of it. All white. I thought it would be easier if I painted all of the walls the same color."

"I have Saturday afternoon off," he said. "I'll come by and take care of it."

"I'm home at two."

"Then we'll do it then," he promised, wondering if he should talk about getting married now or wait until the day after tomorrow. Of course, he didn't intend to let her paint. Inhale those chemical fumes? Not in her condition. This pregnancy thing was complicated. He'd discovered there were dangers everywhere—in alcohol and tobacco, caffeine, hair dye, chemicals and even a cat's litter box. "You don't have a cat, do you?"

"No. I'm a dog person." She yawned with her hand over her mouth. "Do you have a dog?"

"Not at the moment. I'm still living in the Good Times motel outside of town." Which he hoped would change soon. He'd sleep on the couch here if he had to, but he was damn determined to be there for Lorna when his son was born.

"That's a terrible-looking place."

"It's not that bad. I've looked at some places to rent, but what I really want to do is buy back my ranch from Bobby Calhoun. He bought it after the divorce."

"Come on," she said, turning to leave the room. "You can tell me all about it from a sitting position."

It was an odd little house, he realized. The small hallway led past the kitchen and into another room that blended into the living room at the front of the house.

"This should be the dining room," she said, "but I think I'll keep it empty until I decide if I need a dining room or not."

"Is there an upstairs?"

"There is, but it's not finished. Aunt Carol used it for storage." She sat on the couch and leaned back, but Jess didn't take the opposite chair. Instead he sat at the other end of the couch.

"Lie down," he said. "You can put your feet in my lap." The book had said that elevating the legs helped with—he couldn't remember what it helped with—but it was easy enough to do once she stretched out and relaxed.

"That's nice," she said. "But my shoes are dirty and I don't want to get your pants—"

"I'll take off your shoes." He untied the laces and slipped them off her white-stockinged feet. Then he tossed the shoes to the floor while Lorna wiggled her toes and sighed. Jess repositioned her feet so that her toes weren't touching his crotch. She didn't need to know that her touch elicited an immediate response from the lower part of his body.

"That feels so much better," she said, fixing a pillow behind her head. Lorna reached up and pulled the elastic from her ponytail and let her hair tumble down around her face before she closed her eyes. "Okay. Now you can tell me about your dog."

"I don't have a dog," he said.

"You used to. What kind?"

"A hairy black mutt named Bones. That's when I was a kid."

"Now tell me about your ranch," she said, her eyes still closed. Her toes wiggled and he absentmindedly took one foot in between his hands and began to rub.

"It's a small place," he said. "It's pretty close to the Dead Horse, where Bobby Calhoun lives. Do you know him?"

"Everyone knows him," she said. "A sweet guy but a little wild."

"Yeah, that's Calhoun. He bought my place when I had to sell out, but he said he'd be glad to lease it to me or sell it to me whenever I wanted." Jess took her other foot and began rubbing that, too. She had tiny little feet and delicate ankles.

"That was nice of him."

"He's got more money than he knows what to do with, but with Jake gone—Jake used to be his foreman before he got married—Bobby can't seem to stop doing wild things."

"He goes out with a lot of girls. They talk about it at the café. So when are you going to buy your ranch?"

"Soon," he said, realizing that he damn well better do it before he and Lorna got married or else it would be community property again. Another divorce and another For Sale sign wasn't much to look forward to. He'd have to call Calhoun tomorrow and hope that he was sober enough to talk business. He could live out at the ranch for now, and maybe even after the wedding. There was no guarantee Lorna would invite him to move in with her. He stifled a groan. Now that would sure give the town something to talk about.

But one thing at a time, and now it was time to get another marriage proposal over with. Maybe the rings would tip the odds in his favor this time. Jess took a deep breath.

"I figure I've been going about this all the wrong way," he told Lorna.

"Going about what?" she asked. Her eyes were

closed and her toes were no longer moving. Exhaustion was obviously getting the better of her.

"This marriage business," he replied, resting his head against the back of the couch. He looked into the empty room that should be a dining room and wondered if he and Lorna would have friends over for dinner. He didn't know if she liked to cook or if she liked having company. He didn't know if she planned to work after the baby came or if she wanted to stay home. She'd lived in Dallas and worked in a fancy department store. Would she be happy living in Beauville? Would she want fancy clothes and fancy shoes and fancy furniture and shop for his son at Baby Gap?

Jess fought down his panic. He and Lorna needed to agree on things, that was all. She seemed like a reasonable woman. He sure as hell wouldn't mind sharing her bed and he liked the way she looked and the way she felt when he touched her and that scent of vanilla on her skin when she'd finished taking a bath. She hadn't yelled at him or called him names, hadn't complained that he never listened to her or that he worked too many hours.

But none of that mattered, not when there was a baby on the way. Not when there was *his* baby on the way. Although, he had to admit that in the dark moments of the night, he wondered if this really was his baby. It could be anyone's, he worried. Even Texas

Tom's. Lorna could have set him up, or she might even be convincing herself the child was his when it really wasn't. He didn't know much about her past, except for what she told him, and the fact that she'd had no arrests or traffic violations in the state of Texas.

Not too many people he knew could say that, except maybe eighty-nine-year-old Gert Knepper and he didn't even know if the woman knew how to drive.

Jess turned his head and gazed at the woman he had to marry. She was asleep, her breathing soft and even, her hands folded neatly on top of her rounded abdomen. No, the only thing she'd asked him to do was pick up a crib in Marysville. Everything else he'd offered. And then, when she'd refused, he'd done it anyway.

He had only himself to blame.

"WELL, IS IT official yet?" Chelsea greeted her boss with a cup of coffee and a list of his messages.

"Is what official?"

"The engagement. Did you give her the ring?"

"No." He took the coffee and ignored the messages. "Thanks," he said, taking a sip. He'd overslept and hadn't had time to stop for his usual coffee at the café this morning.

Chelsea, her platinum hair pulled back from her

face with rhinestone barrettes, followed him to his desk. "Why not?"

"She fell asleep."

"You've got to brush up on your romantic technique, boss."

"She's six months pregnant, Chelsea. The woman gets tired."

"Well, it's not like you have all the time in the world, you know." She dropped the pile of messages in front of him and he saw that her fingernails were silver with little cowboy boots painted on them. "Bobby Calhoun, Jake Johnson, Marysville sheriff's office, the courthouse, and the animal shelter."

"Any emergencies?"

"Not that I know of. Carter's log from last night didn't show anything but a car alarm going off on Main Street and some kids fooling around in the parking lot behind the library."

"Good. I'll take care of these," he said, leafing through the blue slips of paper, but Chelsea lingered at his desk.

"Is Bobby Calhoun coming into town today?"

"I'm going out there. Why? You joining his long list of girlfriends?" He eyed her over the rim of his coffee cup. "I thought you had more sense."

"Are *you* trying to give *me* dating advice, Jess?"

"Never in a million years," he declared. "How the hell am I supposed to propose to that woman again?"

"Again?"

"Don't ask," he said.

"How many times have you asked? Two? Three?"

"Forget I said anything. Please."

"Just show her the ring, Sheriff. The rest will take care of itself." She reached over for the carafe and refilled his coffee cup. "And hurry up. Everyone's asking me when the wedding's going to be."

"Chelsea," he said, holding her gaze with what he hoped was his meanest and most threatening expression. "Do I look like I want the whole town to know my business?"

"Uh, no, but you can't blame people for asking. It's all anybody can talk about."

Great. Now all of Beauville knew about the wedding before the bride did.

LORNA LOOKED UP every time the café door jangled and someone else walked in. Jess hadn't shown up for coffee this morning and she realized she'd started looking for him around seven-thirty.

She'd awakened in the middle of the night to go to the bathroom and discovered she'd fallen asleep on the couch. Jess was gone, the house empty. He'd covered her with a lightweight blanket he must have found in her bedroom closet.

"This marriage business," he'd said. "All wrong." She wished she could remember more. Wished he'd still been there when she woke up so he could explain what he meant.

The trouble was, Lorna realized, as she poured coffee and served plates of eggs and bacon, French toast and pancakes, that she was falling in love with Jess Sheridan all over again. But this time it wasn't the crush of a young girl admiring the high school athlete. It wasn't the "right place at the right time" magic that happened last summer when she'd awakened to find herself against Jess Sheridan's very strong and very naked body. This time Lorna was very afraid she was falling in love for real. With a man who insisted upon taking care of his child and that child's mother. Who cared enough to meet her doctor, who bossed her into getting more rest, who bought her ice cream and rubbed her aching feet.

"I didn't order pancakes," Mike said, handing his plate back to her. "I'm scrambled eggs and bacon."

"I've got your eggs," the man two stools down from him called. Lorna helped them trade plates while she apologized. Falling in love again with Jess Sheridan didn't mean she had to act stupid. Her baby needed a mother who paid attention. And, she realized, a father Lorna could trust to care for both of them.

"Lorna!"

"What?"

"You've got four orders getting cold up here. What the heck's going on?"

"Sorry, Charlie. It's a little busy here this morning."

He peered out of the serving window. "Not anymore than usual for a Friday."

Lorna managed to deliver the breakfasts without mixing up the orders, but it wasn't easy. She realized she hadn't given Jess the receipt for the crib, so if he went all the way to Marysville to pick it up they wouldn't give it to him. When she refilled the coffee machine she remembered that her new rocking chair was still at Emily's house. Elizabeth's influence had resulted in three pregnant women heading home with three antique rocking chairs tied onto the roof of the car.

"Lorna!" Charlie sounded like he was about to lose his temper, so Lorna stopped refilling coffee cups for the customers along the counter and turned around.

"What?"

"The coffee machine," he yelled. "You didn't put the pot back in!"

"Oh, no," she cried when she saw the coffee dripping all over the back counter. She grabbed a thick dish towel to mop up the mess and burned her fingers on the scalding coffee spraying from underneath the basket. Charlie came around from the back and turned off the machine while Lorna held her fingers under cold running water at the sink. Various suggestions came from the customers, but Lorna knew that cold water worked best, for now, and if she needed anything else she could find something in Charlie's first aid kit under the counter.

The problem, of course, was that folks were going to have to wait a few more minutes before they got fresh coffee. And Texans liked their coffee.

And Charlie liked his customers to be happy and his waitress to be efficient. So when the cook frowned and the customers groaned, Lorna blinked back tears, dried her hand carefully with a paper towel, and helped Charlie clean up the mess. She reassembled the coffee machine, told the guys at the counter that she was fine and continued to clear empty plates. When the new pot of coffee was ready, she refilled cups throughout the restaurant, until the carafe ran dry. The back of her right hand stung and throbbed, but Lorna ignored it. It was her own fault, daydreaming about Jess when she should have been concentrating on her work. Next time the door jangled, she didn't look up hoping that Jess would walk through the door.

Twenty minutes later she started looking again. So when Mike Monterro said, "Your boyfriend's here," she spun around to see. He waved to the sheriff. "You can have this seat, Sheriff. I've got errands to do this morning."

Lorna tried not to show her surprise. It would be the first time she'd known the old man to leave before ten.

"Thanks," Jess said, and the old man winked at him before leaving his money on the counter and picking up his cap.

"Coffee?" she asked, poised to fill a clean mug.

"I've had enough," Jess said, looking stern and tired and very, very determined. Lorna carefully put the carafe back where it belonged and then turned to ask him if he wanted breakfast.

"There's a pancake special," she said, having no idea if he liked pancakes or not.

"No, thanks," Jess said.

She lowered her voice because she knew darn well everyone wanted to hear what she and Jess had to say to each other. Even Charlie had stopped banging pans and he loved banging pans—said it made him feel like a real chef. "I'm sorry about last night. About falling asleep while you were talking."

"Probably won't be the last time," he said. "Could I have some coffee, Lorna?"

"I thought you said you'd had enough."

"I wasn't talking about coffee. I've had enough—" He stopped. "What happened to your hand?"

"A little problem with the coffee machine. My fault," she admitted. "I wasn't paying attention."

"I've got something for that at the office."

"It's fine, really," Lorna insisted, flustered when he took gentle hold of her wrist to look at the red burns. "Do you want coffee? I'm getting confused."

"Confused isn't the half of it," Charlie grumbled. He came out from the kitchen with plates of food on a tray. "She's a walking accident today." He delivered breakfast to a nearby booth of cowboys as Lorna watched. She knew she should feel guilty but she didn't. Not really.

"Charlie really needs to hire more help," she said, turning back to Jess. He hadn't let go of her wrist, so she assumed that a cup of coffee wasn't high on his list of priorities right now. "What's going on, Jess?"

"I'm going to have to arrest you," he muttered. "Come on." He released her wrist and called over to the cook. "I'm taking your waitress in for questioning," he said, and the café fell silent.

"Are you crazy?" she asked. "Questioning for what?"

"Come along, miss," he said, using his official tone. "We'll discuss this at the station."

"I can't leave right now," Lorna said, but Jess winked at her. So she grabbed her purse and walked around the counter, past the cash register and over to the sheriff.

"Oh, for cripe's sake," Charlie grumbled. "You can't leave me like this."

Jess paused before opening the door. "You want to be charged with interfering with a police officer?"

"You're not fooling anyone," the cook grumbled. The cowboys in a nearby booth gave Lorna the thumbs-up sign and an elderly lady drinking tea waved. "Don't bring her back," the cook called. "She's useless today anyway."

"Charlie's going to fire me for this."

"No, he's not, because you're going to quit." He motioned toward the truck. "Get in. We have to make a quick stop at the office first and put something on those burns."

She started to protest that she wasn't going to quit her job, but thought better about arguing that point. The truth was, she didn't know how much longer she could keep up this pace. Or how much longer she could resist loving Jess Sheridan. "Okay," she said. And that's what she would say the next time he talked about getting married.

Jess didn't love her—and maybe he never would—but it was time to stop thinking of what she couldn't have and start thinking about what was best for her daughter. She and Jess would love their child, and maybe that would have to be enough for all three of them.

9

HE KICKED Chelsea out of the office and sent her over to the café to console Charlie who, Jess had finally figured out, was a cousin's second husband, not to be confused with the cousin due to give birth the same time as Lorna, Chelsea explained.

"I'll be back in twenty minutes," the secretary said. "You have an appointment with Bobby at two. He called back to say he'd meet you at your old place. And, boss?"

"Hmm?"

"Remember what I said." *Show her the ring,* she mouthed behind Lorna's back.

Jess nodded and pointed toward the door, but his secretary paid no attention. Instead she called to Lorna, "Don't worry about the café. Charlie has three nieces who are dying to make money to pay off Christmas bills. I'll remind Charlie and get help for him for the rest of the day."

"The rest of the day?" Lorna looked as if she couldn't believe her luck. "Thank you."

"Bye," Chelsea called on her way out of the room. "Have fun."

Fun? Proposing to Lorna for the fourth time wasn't his idea of fun. Jess delayed the question by opening a closet and finding the medication to put on Lorna's hand. "Here," he said, sounding gruffer than he wanted to. "Sit down in my chair. This will help."

"Good. It's beginning to sting," she admitted. "It was such a stupid thing to have done."

"How'd it happen?" He perched on the edge of the desk and opened the jar. He dipped his index finger into the cream, then very carefully applied it to the burn marks on her hand.

"I was daydreaming and didn't put the carafe under the coffee machine. You should have seen the mess."

"Maybe it's time to stop working so hard." He released her hand and waited for the argument.

"Maybe it is."

Well, that was encouraging news. "Really?"

"Yes. I've been really tired lately," she admitted. "I guess you've noticed. I'm sorry about last night, but I never knew how relaxing it was to have my feet rubbed."

"I'm not a romantic man," Jess said, and she looked up at him with those big blue eyes that never failed to make him want to kiss her. He took a deep breath and resisted the sudden erotic visions of Lorna in his bed. "I'm not going to tell you I love you or promise things I can't deliver. When I make promises

I keep them. And whether you marry me or not, I promise to help you support our child."

"Jess—" she began.

"Hear me out, Lorna. I don't think it's right for a kid to grow up without a father, especially if a perfectly good one is volunteering for the job, but if you're that set against marriage I sure can't drag you to a judge—even if it's damn tempting—and make you say 'I do.'"

"But I do."

"What?"

"I do," she repeated. "You don't have to drag me anywhere," she said. "You're right."

"I am?" If that was true, this could be a pretty damn good day. Jess leaned forward.

"We're in this together," Lorna said, still looking at him with those eyes that said, "Take me to bed and do it fast." "And I've begun to realize that I need—" She hesitated.

"Help?" he supplied.

"You." She shrugged, as if she didn't understand it herself. "Just you." She smiled then. "*And* some help getting the baby's room ready."

Jess took a deep breath and then exhaled. He didn't expect to feel such staggering relief. This woman was going to marry him. He should want to run to Mexico and hide until his kid was eighteen, but instead he felt as if he'd been given some kind of special gift. "What made you change your mind?"

She hesitated. "I'm not sure."

Jess could tell she wasn't telling the truth, but he didn't push his luck. This wasn't the time for an interrogation. According to all the advice he'd been given, this was the time for jewelry. He leaned over and opened his desk drawer. Retrieving a gray velvet pouch, he said, "Hold out your hands."

"Jess?" She looked stunned, but she did as he'd asked, and he poured the contents into her cupped fingers. She gasped as three rings landed in her hands.

"They belonged to my grandmother," he explained. "I thought you could pick the one you liked best, or if you don't like any of them we can go over to Joe's and see if there's something there you like better."

Lorna held the three rings in her left hand and picked up the platinum band with the three large diamonds set in something that looked like little flowers. She set it carefully on the desk and then selected the gold ring with the large blue stone—he thought he remembered his grandmother calling it an "aquamarine"—that was a shade lighter than Lorna's eyes.

"Lorna?" Her silence shook him. He'd never shown Sue the rings; he'd mentioned them to her, but she'd insisted on something of her own that no one had ever worn before. He didn't think Lorna would feel the same way—she didn't seem to mind living in her Aunt Carol's house and none of the furniture looked at all new—but he could be wrong. He'd been wrong as hell about lots of things in the past years.

She didn't answer. The remaining ring was also platinum, but looked more like a wedding band. Tiny diamonds, caught in the sunlight coming in the window near Jess's desk, sparkled along the front of the ring.

Jess started to sweat. He didn't know Lorna well, but he sure didn't think of her as the silent type.

"Say something," he demanded, wishing he knew more about rings. And more about women, too. "Are they too old-fashioned? The wrong color? What?"

"I'm sorry," she whispered, setting the third ring next to the others on the desk blotter. She wiped her eyes with her fingers and looked up at him. "They're all very beautiful."

"Then what's the matter?"

"My fingers are too swollen." She gave him a lopsided smile. "I know it's a silly thing to cry about, but they're never going to fit me. Not until after the baby's born."

"We'll get them resized."

"I'm just going to swell up more, I think." She picked up each ring and put them back in the pouch, then handed it to him. "Put them away, Jess."

"They're all yours," he said, disappointed, "if you want them."

"They were gifts of love," Lorna said. "The platinum rings look like an engagement ring and a wedding band. It doesn't seem right because—"

"Because we don't love each other," he finished for her. "What's that got to do with anything?"

"I'll wait for a while," she said. "Until it feels right."

He tossed the pouch in the desk drawer. "Have it your way, but I know my grandmother wouldn't have minded a bit. She was a practical woman."

"Not with rings like those."

"Platinum is stronger than gold, I believe," Jess said, helping Lorna to her feet. "The aquamarine is a little flashy, but Grandma liked to wear it to church."

"Your grandma had good taste." She glanced at the clock. "I should get back to work."

Over his dead body. "Chelsea was going to take care of that for you. You have no idea how efficient she is. Take the rest of the day off."

"I *could* get a lot of things done in the baby's room," she said.

He handed her the phone. "Call the café and find out." While she did just that, Jess checked his schedule. Officially, he had the afternoon off because he was working tonight. He didn't want Lorna getting "a lot of things done" this afternoon. She'd probably paint a ceiling and sand floors and Lord only knew what else.

They would head north and pick up the crib. He would make sure she ate a healthy lunch. They would discuss the when and where of getting married.

Jess left a note for Chelsea. He was going to Marysville instead of the Triple Bar S. Buying back his ranch could wait a while longer. And from the size of Lorna, getting married couldn't.

"IT'S NEXT FRIDAY," Chelsea declared as she hung up the phone. "At four-thirty."

"What is?" Carter didn't look away from his monitor. The dope was playing solitaire.

"The boss's wedding. It's supposed to be a big secret, of course. He didn't even write it in his appointment book." Men thought they were so smart, Chelsea mused. The sheriff didn't know that she went to high school with one of the clerks at the courthouse. Debbie still owed Chelsea a favor for covering for her the night in 1996 when she and her boyfriend drove to Austin for the Garth Brooks concert.

"So? You know he doesn't talk much."

"We're giving them a party, remember? I have everyone standing by."

"He's not going to like it," Carter warned.

"Lorna will."

Carter shrugged as if to say he wasn't going to argue with her.

"We're inviting everyone in town," Chelsea said. "I'll bet Mandy and Sandy Wynette will come." That made him perk up. The idiot didn't know the twins were too young for him and if they added the Wynette brain cells together there still wouldn't be enough to compare to a jackrabbit's.

"I can't picture Jess going along with this," the deputy said, drumming his fingers on the desk. "He could get really ticked off. Someone could get fired and it better not be me."

"We'll keep it simple," Chelsea promised. "Wedding cake and champagne at the Grange, so the new Mr. and Mrs. Sheridan have a wedding to remember."

"The sheriff already had a wedding to remember. He went to Jake Johnson's and that's why he's in the mess he is now."

"Weddings are romantic," Chelsea insisted. "And romance is contagious."

Carter frowned at her. "Yeah, well, if that's true, I'm making sure I don't drink too much and I keep my pants zipped."

"That's always a good idea," Chelsea agreed, hiding her laughter. "Especially when the Wynettes are around."

"THIS IS THE STRANGEST wedding party I've ever seen," Emily declared. "We look like an advertisement for fertility drugs."

"I'm glad you're both here." Lorna glanced into the full-length mirror on the back of her closet door. Her ivory linen maternity dress didn't conceal her advanced state of pregnancy, but it did make her look elegant. She'd fixed her hair in a loose topknot and attached three ivory silk rosebuds into the curls.

Elizabeth wore a fashionably loose butterscotch dress that hinted at her pregnancy, but to her disappointment she wasn't close to wearing maternity clothes yet. And Emily, in a sage green suit, looked more than almost five months along.

"It's my fourth," she'd explained to an envious Elizabeth. "My body automatically pops into position. Lorna, you look beautiful."

"For a whale." No matter how dressed up she was, she couldn't hide her giant abdomen. "Brides are supposed to look radiant," she said, turning to see her profile, which was even more depressing. "I look pale."

"You're radiant," Elizabeth assured her.

"I've been getting more rest now that I'm not working anymore."

"It's more than that, Lorna," her new friend insisted. "Anyone can see that you and Jess are crazy about each other."

"He's only marrying me because of the baby," she said. "We all know that."

"But you're in love with him," Emily pointed out. "That has to count for something."

"I thought it would at first, but I think now that it makes it all so much harder," she admitted. "Maybe he still loves his ex-wife."

"I doubt it." Elizabeth frowned. "Not from what Jake has said."

"I'd like to believe that," Lorna said, but in her heart she knew that Jess had a long way to go before he thought of their marriage as anything but his duty.

"Hey," Emily said. "What are you worried about? You'll have him wrapped around your little finger in no time. You'll be his wife, the woman having his baby and sharing his bed."

"But how do you seduce a husband?" She looked down at her belly and then at her friends. "Especially in this condition. Do you have any advice?"

"You say, 'Come to bed now, honey.' It's that simple." Emily picked up the nosegay from the bed and handed it to Lorna.

Elizabeth chuckled. "Once again, Emily is right."

HE'D KNOWN he would get married. He'd planned to stand up in front of the judge and make his vows. He'd give Lorna and the child his name. He pictured the three of them living in Lorna's comfortable little house for a while, and then on the ranch.

But Jess hadn't let himself think about the wedding night.

And now, twenty minutes before the wedding, the wedding night was all he could think about.

"Jess."

"Yeah?" He stood in the waiting room of the court-house, which, thankfully, was empty except for one curious clerk. Jake clapped him on the shoulder.

"You okay?"

"I'm not sure." He felt short of oxygen, like the time when he'd seen the ultrasound at Dr. Bradford's office. "Thanks for being here."

"No problem." Jake looked at his watch. "George will be here with the women soon. Do you have the license?"

"Yeah." He patted his jacket pocket. "All set."

"And the ring?"

"Yes." Now that had been another problem. Lorna—who had a stubborn streak he hadn't known about—had finally agreed to the purchase of a simple gold band, sized to fit her finger. "If you see a woman who looks like a, uh, mature Shania Twain wandering around, that's my sister. She's coming from Austin."

"I'll keep an eye out for her. What's her name?"

"Ricky. I couldn't contact my folks. I think they're

hiking in the Grand Canyon, but as soon as they hear they're going to be grandparents they'll be back in Texas soon enough." Would they remember Lorna, the girl down the street? He hoped so. It would make it easier for them to accept their son marrying his pregnant girlfriend if they knew there'd been a past connection.

An older man, with a shock of gray hair and startling blue eyes, strolled into the waiting room. He wore a blue Western-cut suit, a turquoise bolero and a white Stetson. He stopped near Jess and Jake and asked, "Which one of you is marrying my daughter?"

"I am, sir," Jess said. He shook the man's hand. "I'm Jess Sheridan." He introduced his best man. "And this is a good friend of mine, Jake Johnson."

"Hank Walters," Lorna's father said. "Call me Hank. Nice to meet you," he said to Jake before studying his future son-in-law. "I wouldn't have recognized you, Sheridan. You've grown."

"Yes, I—"

"Are you going to make my little girl happy?"

"Yes, sir. I'm certainly going to try."

"That's all that matters. That, and taking good care of my grandchild." He beamed. "I expect to visit often, Sheridan."

"You're always welcome." Jess wondered if his son would have to learn to square dance. Probably, unless he was as uncoordinated as his father.

"They're here," Jake announced, and Jess turned around to see Lorna ushered into the waiting room with Elizabeth and the Bennetts. She looked more beautiful than ever, he realized. And he was the luckiest son of a bitch in Texas. All he had to do was say the words he was expected to say and then show some restraint when he kissed her. Jess started toward her, but her father beat him to it and greeted her with a big hug.

"How are you doing, Sheriff?" Emily patted his arm. "Doesn't Lorna look beautiful?"

"She takes my breath away." He didn't dare take his gaze from her for fear she'd change her mind and leave town before she said "I do."

The judge opened the door to his inner office and invited them inside. Jess forgot that he was scared to death and strode over to his bride's side. He took her hand in his and, without realizing what he was doing, brought her hand to his lips.

"You look beautiful," he told her. She smiled up at him with such dazzling happiness, he was nearly blinded. It stunned him to see such happiness on a woman's—*his* woman's—face. As quickly as he'd seen it, the expression was gone, replaced by something more restrained and polite.

"Thank you. Are you sure about this?"

"Yes." He kept careful hold of her left hand as the

judge motioned them closer, but he looked down at his bride once again. "Very sure."

The rest was a blur he looked back on later and tried to remember. The ceremony was brief, the judge austere, and the father of the bride wiped away tears as he stood next to Emily, who gave him a tissue from her purse. Jess continued to hold Lorna's hand until it was time to exchange rings. He'd insisted on his own wedding band, something simple that matched the one she'd selected. The platinum and diamonds would have to wait, but Jess was disappointed that Lorna wouldn't wear them on her wedding day. He wanted the mother of his child to have them.

He wiped the tears from her cheeks before he kissed her. He'd intended to keep the kiss brief, a mere formality, but her tears unsettled him. And when she reached up to touch his arms he kissed her longer than he'd planned. A man should be able to kiss his wife, after all.

Jess shook hands with the men, kissed Elizabeth's cheek and returned Emily's affectionate hug. There. It was over. Now he and Lorna could get on with having a baby.

The young clerk opened the door for them. "Would you exit through the back, please? We've already locked the front doors."

He thought later that he should have suspected something, but Jess was still a little dazed. He took

Lorna's hand once again and kept her beside him as they walked down the hall to the back exit that fronted the park. They were to have dinner at the Johnsons' house, an intimate gathering suited to the occasion, but when Jess stepped outside he heard his sister singing "Here Comes the Bride," her raucous band accompanying her at the foot of the cement steps.

A crowd of well-wishers threw rice and cheered. Ricky, dressed in white leather and rhinestones, blew him a kiss. Chelsea hurried over with a tray filled with glasses of champagne. "We had to have a celebration," she said. "Don't be mad. It's not a wedding without champagne and cake."

Jess looked at Lorna, who didn't seem at all disturbed by the noise, the crowd, the rice, or the singing sister-in-law. In fact, his bride looked absolutely delighted with the idea of a party.

"Come on," Chelsea said to the wedding party gathered behind the bride and groom. "Take a glass of champagne and come over to the Grange. You have to cut the cake."

He guessed the wedding night would have to wait.

10

"WELL," Jess said, loosening his tie as he stood in her living room. "That was unexpected."

"It was really nice of everyone to go to so much trouble." The Grange ladies had supplied a potluck supper; Elizabeth had known all along there was to be no dinner at her ranch and instead brought huge cuts of roasted beef. One of the tables held a three-tier cake, special-ordered from Marysville by Charlie. White and silver balloons and baskets of wildflowers decorated the long tables at the Grange. The paper plates and napkins had been decorated with silver wedding bells and there had even been a table full of wedding gifts. Jess had brought them in and piled them in the middle of the living room.

Lorna eased herself onto the couch and kicked off her shoes. "Your sister can really sing."

Jess grinned and tossed his tie on the back of a chair. The jacket followed. "She's pretty wild, but your father didn't seem to mind."

"Did you see them dancing together?" The band had set up their instruments in one corner of the hall and proceeded to play any song the guests requested. It had been a big night for Patsy Cline songs after the crowd realized Ricky Sheridan could yodel. "My dad had a wonderful time."

"I did, too," Jess admitted. "So Chelsea's job is safe."

"That was sweet of her to go to all that trouble. I saw her dancing with your deputy. What's his name?"

"Jim Carter."

"She likes him."

"Yeah. And he doesn't have a clue." Jess unbuttoned the top two buttons of his shirt and rolled up his sleeves. "Can I get you anything?"

You could take me to bed and make love to me, she wanted to say. *You could pretend I was desirable, even with my basketball belly.* "No. I wish I could have had a glass of champagne."

"I'll bring you some after the baby's born," he promised.

"Will you be there?"

"Do you want me there?"

"I don't want to be alone." She had thought of asking her father, but if anything went wrong he would be too upset to be of any help to her. And Emily, before she knew about Jess, had offered to be her birthing coach.

"Do you want *me* there?" he asked again.

"Yes," she said. "I do."

"Then that's where I'll be." He sat down in the chair opposite her and let out a sigh. "This is a strange honeymoon."

Lorna knew she was being overly sensitive, but she couldn't seem to stop from tearing up. "I'm sorry I'm not exactly the perfect woman for a wedding night. I *want* to be, but it's—"

"Lorna?" Jess left the chair and came to sit beside her on the couch. "I wasn't talking about you. I was thinking that I should have taken you somewhere special so you could have had a honeymoon."

"I'm being ridiculous," she said, but her voice quavered. "I wanted a wedding night and here I am swollen up like an old bullfrog." He put his arm around her and she leaned against his shoulder.

"You're a beautiful bullfrog," he said, and kissed the top of her head. "I like the way you did your hair with the flowers like that."

"Really?"

"And you don't look swollen. You look...ripe. And very beautiful."

If she could only say the words: *Honey, come to bed.* Emily had made it sound so simple. Lorna hadn't thought much about a honeymoon. It wasn't as if they were in love with each other and dying to be alone.

At least one of them wasn't. She couldn't speak for

Jess, but he didn't act like a man who was in love. He acted like a man who was doing his duty and getting it over with.

Oh, he'd been polite, and respectful. And he went through the motions so that no one would ever believe that he wasn't getting married out of love.

Even the kiss at the end of the wedding ceremony must have looked authentic. For a moment even Lorna had forgotten it wasn't. Had even forgotten she'd entered her seventh month of pregnancy.

Lorna took his free hand and placed it on her belly. "Here," she said. "Feel your baby kick."

"You're kidding." His touch was light, as if he was afraid he would hurt her, and he jumped when the baby moved against his palm. "My God. Does he do that a lot?"

"Yes." She loved that he kept his hand on her abdomen, his fingers spread across the fabric of her dress. That was something, even if it didn't exactly qualify as wedding night foreplay. "Especially in the middle of the night."

"Is it hard to sleep?"

"Sometimes." She put her hand over his when he started to withdraw. "Don't," she said. "You might as well start getting to know each other."

"I'm scared to death," Jess muttered.

"Of the baby?"

"Of lots of things." His lips touched her temple,

tickled her ear, kissed a path to her mouth when she turned her face to his. Then he pulled back slightly to say, "This wedding night business is pretty damn scary."

"Should it be?"

"Honey, I've never made love to a pregnant woman before." He smiled down at her before kissing her lips again briefly. "And I don't intend to, so relax, okay? Just because it's our wedding night doesn't mean I'm going to jump your bones."

"Even if I wanted you to?"

"That could change things," he admitted. "I was prepared to show some restraint." Jess kissed a trail along the corner of her mouth to her ear. "Unlike last summer."

"Restraint is overrated." Although, if either one of them had shown any seven months ago, she wouldn't be in this situation right now.

Jess pulled away and looked at her as if he couldn't figure out if she was serious or not. "Honey, are you trying to tell me something?"

She nodded. "Come to bed?"

"I figured I'd sleep on the couch."

"Forever?"

"Well," he hesitated, "I guess I haven't thought that far ahead."

"My mother used to say, 'Begin as you intend to finish.' Or something like that."

"You make your bed, you lie in it?"

"That works, too." She didn't want to admit she'd looked forward to the company in the middle of the night in case something happened. She'd had a few nightmares where she'd dreamed she'd given birth to a Longhorn calf. "I'd like you close by me at night, in case anything happens. In case I need you."

"Sure," he said, as casually as if she'd asked for a drink of water. "Whatever you want."

What she wanted was a husband. A lover. A father for her child. Lorna sighed and Jess left the couch. Maybe she should be content with two out of three.

HOW COULD HE ADMIT he was scared to death? Jess stayed far away from that bedroom while Lorna was getting ready for bed. He'd called the office, half hoping that Carter needed him to break up a brawl, fight a fire or catch a serial killer. Anything would be preferable to lusting after an overtired pregnant woman who trusted him to care for her.

He unpacked the car—the motel had seen the last of him—and took *Words of Wisdom for Expectant Fathers* into the kitchen and read the section on sexual intercourse and "comfortable positions for pregnant lovers" again. Sex at this stage of pregnancy was possible, but not probable. How could a woman want to make love when she had so many other things going on—like another person kicking her while she carried him around twenty-four hours a day?

The book said empathy was very important.

Well, hell, he could be empathetic, and helpful, too. He didn't have to behave like a rutting bull pawing the ground just because Lorna cuddled up to him on the couch. His brand-new wife was trying to be considerate, hinting about a real wedding night, but Jess was too smart to fall for that. He liked Lorna; he wouldn't knowingly do anything to make her think he was only thinking of himself.

He would be strong, Jess vowed. He would take a cold shower and wait for her to fall asleep. And then this damn wedding night would be over.

LORNA INTENDED to seduce her husband if it took all night to do it. She heard the shower water running for what seemed like a long time, heard him thumping about in the bathroom and then in the living room where he'd put his suitcases.

After what seemed like a very long time, Lorna heard him patter softly toward the bed. The nightlight from the bathroom gave a faint glow, enough so that Lorna could see Jess climb into bed. She'd left the left side for him, and when he slipped under the sheet in a very careful and quiet manner, she knew he thought she was asleep. He settled himself on his back and folded his arms under his head as if he planned to stare at the ceiling for a while.

Then, careful to keep her abdomen from touching him, she turned toward him. "Jess?"

"Sorry," he said. "I tried not to wake you."

"You didn't."

"Are you okay?"

"I'm fine. It's hard to go to sleep, though. I keep thinking about the wedding. I wish my father hadn't driven back to Marysville tonight."

"He didn't. Ricky drove him and the band followed in the bus."

"Really?" She moved closer, resting her cheek on his chest. He wore a cotton T-shirt, which was disappointing. But he put his arm around her shoulders, which made up for it.

"I think they were going to party for a while longer."

"He'll wear them out," Lorna said. "The Walters are known for their stamina."

"Like you."

"Like me," she agreed, running her hand across his chest. "Jess?"

"Hmm?" His eyes were closed.

"Will you hold me?"

Silence. For a long moment Lorna held her breath and waited for him to say something. Her hand lay still on his chest.

"Lorna, what are you doing?"

"Trying to seduce my husband."

He swore under his breath, which didn't bode well for any kind of seduction. Or maybe it was the word *husband* he objected to.

"Never mind," she whispered, hoping she wouldn't cry with disappointment. "I understand." With that, she turned away from him and he lifted his arm and let her move away to lie on her side. In a moment she felt the mattress shift as he fumbled with the covers and left the bed. When he returned he faced her back. His fingers brushed her hair away from her cheek.

"Honey, you could tempt a saint," he muttered, his lips close to her ear.

"What about a sheriff?"

"The sheriff took a cold shower and wanted to sleep on the couch." He eased the hem of her nightgown over her hips and higher.

"And now?"

"Now he's going to make love to his wife."

"Oh, good," Lorna sighed as his fingers swept over her bare skin. "I've missed you. Missed this. Even though we only did it once."

"Yes," he said, tucking her against his naked body so she could feel how much he wanted her. No, the sheriff couldn't fake his desire. Lorna sighed with relief. He touched her swollen breasts carefully, his fingers caressing already sensitive nipples. She felt ready to explode by the time he slowly moved lower, over the mound of baby, to find her slippery and open and wanting him inside of her.

She climaxed almost immediately against his exploring fingers, which surprised her and seemed to please him, because after she caught her breath Jess fitted himself inside her as if they'd been lovers for years. The position was surprisingly comfortable. His lips caressed her cheek, his hand held her hip and he made love to her as if she didn't look at all like a bullfrog.

THE NEXT MORNING she made him breakfast, much to Jess's discomfort. He thought she'd be tired after everything that happened on Friday, but he was the one who slept late.

And they both seemed awkward, with the memory of last night between them. Jess didn't know how to behave. Should he act like a husband and kiss her good morning? Should he act like a lover and tuck her against his body while he nuzzled her neck? Or should he behave as if this was one of the bed and breakfast inns and sit down and act polite and talk about the weather?

He picked polite. Less trouble to get into that way.

"This looks real good," he said when she put the plate of food in front of him.

"Do you have to work today?" she asked him, once she'd joined him at the kitchen table. The scrambled eggs, bacon, toast and coffee looked more appetizing here in this house than they did at the café.

"No. I took the weekend off, but I'm still on call if Carter needs me."

"I feel a little guilty leaving Charlie on such short notice," she admitted. "I hope his nieces work out okay."

"Chelsea assures me that everything will be fine." He took a sip of coffee and tried to forget about how responsive she had been last night. He'd never quite experienced anything like it. Maybe marriage to this woman wasn't going to be such a hardship after all.

At least they had passion in common. Put the two of them in a bed together and something was bound to happen, all right. If he wasn't careful he'd end up with six kids in six years, with more on the way.

If he wasn't careful he'd end up falling in love with her, which would be stupid. He barely knew her. They were friends, sort of. That was enough for now. He'd eased his conscience by putting that ring on her finger. She'd gained the chance to stay home from work and raise her child without worrying about where the money to support them was going to come from.

"I imagine you want to spend some time moving in," Lorna said.

"I don't have much." Any furniture that Sue didn't want was most likely still at the ranch. He finished his breakfast and searched for another topic of conversation. "So," he said, racking his brain. "Do you want to go shopping for anything?"

"I don't think so. There's plenty of food and I want to get the baby's room ready before I buy any more baby things."

"I'll set up the crib."

"Thank you. That would be nice."

The silence descended upon them. Jess cleared the table, Lorna loaded the dishwasher and they only bumped into each other twice.

Both times he wished he could carry her off to bed. He would have liked to have known if last night was just a fluke, or did the two of them share some special magic that made sex an extraordinary experience?

He resolved to keep his hands to himself. She was pregnant. He was no horny youth who couldn't control himself. Sex from now on was out of the question, he told himself. But he was going to look in that parenthood book and see how long a man had to wait after the baby was born. He sure as hell didn't know how he was going to make it 'til April.

IF EVER THERE WAS a reminder of what loving a woman could do to a man, it was the Triple Bar S ranch. When Jess drove into his former home and saw what lousy condition the place was in, he wanted to put his head on the steering wheel and curse the gods of Happily Ever After. He would have, but he didn't, because Lorna sat beside him on the front seat of the car.

The place was a disaster. And the problem was neglect, pure and simple. Hell, Jess had had a hard enough time keeping up with the chores when he lived here.

Calhoun had used the land to run cattle, but ignored the two-story house. A year and a half without a tenant had taken its toll on the old place. Part of the roof sagged, paint peeled from the trim boards, and someone had left bags of garbage on the front porch that animals had ripped apart and spread around. It was an older house, from the 1940s, but he'd always thought it was solid.

"I should have come out here sooner," he told his new wife. "But I wanted to wait until I'd talked to Calhoun." He laughed, but nothing was funny. "I didn't want to see it until I knew I could buy it."

Lorna didn't say anything right away. She peered out the windows of the truck at the tree that had fallen against one of the outbuildings he'd once used for storage. "Was it hit by a tornado?"

"Could have been," he admitted, but that explanation was just too damn easy.

"Are you upset?"

He shrugged, knowing denying it would be a lie. All those years he'd worked this place and here it was, as if nobody had ever given a damn about it. "Calhoun was supposed to meet me here at ten," he said, turning off the car engine. "I guess we could get out and wait for him."

"I'll wait here for now," Lorna said, avoiding his gaze.

"Suit yourself." Jess switched the ignition on, rolled down the electric windows, and turned the engine off once again. So here he was, with another woman who couldn't stand the sight of the place. Not that he could blame her, but Lorna didn't know how much this place had meant to him.

He'd known Sue Miller almost his entire life. He hadn't expected any surprises from their marriage; they'd dated throughout high school and after. They'd lost their virginity together the night of the Senior Prom, they'd studied for exams and shared popcorn at the movies. Marriage had seemed inevitable, and Jess had expected to teach his sons how to care for the ranch he would build for his family.

Only there had been no sons. And Susan hadn't been happy living on the ranch, so she'd taken a job in a bank in Marysville and bought a new car and left the ranch every morning at seven and quit talking to her husband.

Three years ago his wife had fallen in love with

someone else, a man she met while at work. Two years ago she'd explained her unhappiness with their marriage and her affair with another man. She'd said it was "love at first sight" and she "couldn't help" herself. And she hoped he would understand.

Jess hadn't understood one damn thing. He'd worked hard to make a life for them and now, looking at his former home, he wondered, not for the first time, why the hell he'd bothered.

And why he would put any energy into doing it again.

"Jess?"

He turned around. "What?"

"Your pager's going off."

"Damn," he muttered, and walked back to the car where his very new and very pregnant wife sat waiting. When he answered the page and Chelsea told him that Bobby Calhoun was running late, he told her to cancel the appointment. He'd reschedule another day, when Lorna wasn't with him.

He'd fix it up, then show it to her again. It would look better a few months from now, he just knew it.

Sort of.

"YOU SHOULDN'T BE spending your honeymoon with your father." Hank winked at her to show he was only kidding. Lorna knew he was thrilled when she, Jess and Ricky accepted his invitation to go out for dinner. She was certainly pleased not to have to spend the evening alone with her very nervous husband. Jess acted as if he was afraid to get too close to her for fear she'd drag him into the bedroom.

"I don't get to see you enough," Lorna told him. "You're a busy man these days."

"Not as busy as your husband." He nodded toward the door of the Steak Barn, where Jess was deep in conversation with his deputy. It must be something important, Lorna knew, because Carter looked worried and Jess had been surprised that the man showed up during dinner.

"If I was fifteen years younger," Ricky Sheridan drawled, "I'd go after that."

"After Carter?" Lorna had always thought the young man was a little dense. Every morning the Coffee Pot breakfast menu confused him. She didn't know how he managed to fight crime and protect Beauville.

"Was he at the wedding reception yesterday?" Ricky asked. "Surely I would have noticed."

"And broken an old man's heart," Hank declared, winking at the singer. "Who would have danced with me if you were flirting with the handsome deputy?"

"The matrons were checking you out, Hank," Ricky told him. "I saw them. I'll bet you don't have to worry about dates."

"Well—" He chuckled. "I do okay. Lorna, honey, are you feeling okay?"

She smiled wanly. "I'm fine." Except that her husband hadn't spoken two words to her since the trip to his former home. She shouldn't have gone with him, even though he'd asked her. He'd looked at that place like his heart was as broken as the roof on one of those little white buildings.

"Maybe we shouldn't come back to the house after dinner," her father suggested. "Maybe you should go home and go to bed nice and early."

"Oh, no," Lorna said. "I want you to come. Ricky hasn't seen the house and there are all those wedding presents to open." And she wasn't sure she wanted to be alone with Jess right away. From the time she'd awakened, Jess had seemed distant. As if last night's lovemaking had never happened. As if eating breakfast together was just too intimate for him. He'd kept his distance and hurt her feelings, but she didn't intend to let him know how much. She had her pride.

"I have a present for the baby, too." Her new sister-in-law grinned. "I can't believe I'm finally going to be an auntie. I never thought Jess would get around to having kids. I never even thought he'd ever get married again, not after the first time."

The first time he had a ranch and a wife he loved. Now he had nothing but a wreck of a ranch house and a wife he'd married out of duty. If Lorna could have crawled under the table and bawled her eyes out, she would have. Only the problem of how to get down on her hands and knees stopped her. That, and the fact that her father and Ricky would have joined her in order to find out what was wrong. And how could she tell them that she was crying because she had fallen in love with her husband?

And Jess, hurrying back to their dinner table, would have felt it was his obligation to make everything better.

"What's wrong?" Ricky asked her brother.

"Not much. We've got some bikers in town," he said, pulling out his chair and sitting down beside Lorna. "Carter's going to keep an eye on them and make sure we don't have any trouble."

"He's cute," his sister said. "Is he married?"

"My secretary has her eye on him," Jess informed her. "I'm not sure she's making progress though."

"Chelsea seems like the kind of person who gets exactly what she wants," Lorna said. "She's fearless."

"She's bossy," her husband countered. "And don't worry, I won't forget to thank her again for the wedding party."

"I know." The man always did the right thing, no matter what the cost. Which was why he wore a wedding band on the third finger of his left hand. She stared at it and wondered what he thought when he looked at it. Did he resent being married again? Did he wish she were Susan Miller?

"Lorna?" She looked up to find her father's gaze on her.

"Yes?"

"Do you want dessert or anything?"

She shook her head. "No, thanks, Daddy."

"Then we'll take you home." He looked at Jess. "Do you have to go anywhere right now?"

"No."

"Then we'd better get Lorna home," Hank told him. "She's looking a mite peaked."

"I am?"

"Yes, honey." He waved the waitress over and asked for the check. "Maybe you've had too much excitement for one weekend."

Lorna blushed and avoided looking at her husband. They hadn't talked about last night. In fact, they hadn't said much to each other all day except for polite questions and answers regarding food, where Jess should store his things, and the weather. She wanted to tell him how much she loved him. She would rather cut out her tongue than actually say the words and become an object of pity. She glanced toward her husband again and wished he weren't so damn handsome.

"You're so lucky, Jess," Lorna heard Ricky sigh. "I

wish someone would look at me the way Lorna looks at you, like you hung the moon over Texas."

Now would be another good time to dive under the table. Or poke her eyes out with the unused dessert fork. Jess didn't want her love. He wanted a ranch. A ranch that had belonged to his first wife, the foolish woman who'd run off with another man and broken her husband's heart.

"Come on." Jess didn't reply to his sister's comment. Instead he stood and helped Lorna to her feet. "You wanted to open the wedding gifts tonight."

"Yes." She would open wedding presents and pretend that everything was okay. At least until the baby was born.

And then she'd have to rethink this whole mess.

11

"Is it normal to want to cry all the time?"

Emily considered the question and took another sip of iced tea. They sat on Lorna's front porch and watched little Elly dig a hole in the flower beds by the stairs. "Well, yes, if we're talking about pregnancy," she said, but her concerned expression deepened. "No, if we're talking about marriage. Are you crying a *lot*, Lorna?"

"Not a lot." Which she knew didn't sound convincing.

"You've been married a week," her friend said. "Should I ask how it's going?"

Lorna took a deep breath and thought about the past seven days with her new husband. "He put the crib together," she said. "It only took about five hours."

"Not bad," Emily smiled, "for a sheriff."

"And he sent me out of the house for three hours while he painted the baby's room. He'd read that paint fumes could be harmful to pregnant women, so I went to the library and looked at decorating magazines."

"Okay. So far so good."

"Last Saturday, the day after we got married, he drove me out to his ranch, the one he used to live on with his first wife."

"Uh-oh."

"No kidding." Lorna leaned back in her chair and rested her hands on her belly. The baby was kicking a lot more lately, as if she was anxious to get out into the world. "It was a very big 'uh-oh.' The place looked pretty terrible, but it was obvious that he loved it."

"Does he want to live there again?"

"I think so. We haven't talked about it since then, but I know he wants to talk to Bobby Calhoun about buying the place back from him." And then her eyes filled up with those embarrassing tears. Lorna reached into her shirt pocket for a tissue, just in case they overflowed. "He still loves his wife, Em."

"No way," her loyal friend declared. "Absolutely no way."

"No, it's true," Lorna insisted. "Why else would he want his ranch back? Wouldn't you think it would have bad memories?"

"I don't think men think the same way we do about things like this," Emily warned. "I think he looks at that ranch and just sees...a ranch."

"Maybe so, but that doesn't change that he only married me because I was pregnant." Darn. The tears spilled over, so Lorna wiped them away as quickly as she could.

"Oh, Lorna," Emily said. "Are you sure? Pregnancy really does make us more emotional."

"I'm sure," she declared. "We slept together one night last summer, which was a stupid thing to do, but believe me, neither one of us was thinking clearly at the time. I didn't want to fall in love with him then and I didn't want to fall in love with him now, but I did and I am and—" she paused to wipe her nose "—and I shouldn't."

"Your baby is going to need a father," Emily said. "And you've married a good man for the job. If he doesn't already love you, he will soon enough." She smiled. "How could he help it? You're gorgeous and you adore him. That's a pretty potent combination."

"You think?"

"I'm positive. Just give it time."

Lorna looked down at her expanding belly. "We only have nine weeks left," she said. "I hope that's time enough."

"HOW'S IT GOING, boss?" Chelsea perched on the edge of his desk and tapped her index finger on his appointment book. "Got anything in there I should enter in the computer?"

"Like what?" He'd been sitting in front of the same files for two hours and hadn't accomplished a damn thing. Lorna had been too quiet all week and he couldn't figure out what was wrong with her. Was she regretting getting married already?

"Like Lorna's checkup tomorrow at three o'clock with Dr. Bradford."

"That's personal." He hoped they wouldn't use that ultrasound machine again. Maybe it was easier to watch the second time. He sure as hell hoped so.

"Valentine's Day is only ten days away. You don't want to forget candy and flowers."

"Right." Yeah. He'd look like a jerk carrying flowers and candy to a woman who was barely speaking to him. It was the ranch, he figured. Or the sex. He knew he shouldn't have made love to her, knew he shouldn't have reacted to her offer to make love on their wedding night.

God, he'd wanted her. And still did. Which made him feel like a pervert. He'd slept beside her all week and he'd made sure to keep on his side of the bed. He'd tried hard not to inhale the enticing scent of her hair or brush against any exposed skin. He set his alarm for five, so that he and his erection could get out of bed before waking Lorna.

"Jess."

He looked up at Chelsea again. "What?"

"You're not listening to a word I'm saying."

"No," he agreed. "I'm not. Sorry. Try me again." He tossed his pen down and leaned back in his chair.

He wished he could prop his boots up on the desk, but he'd be sure to knock over the files and then have to spend another three hours putting them in order. Carter walked in and hung his hat by the door.

"Hey," he said. "How's it goin'?"

"Hey," Jess said. It was as much of a greeting as Carter expected. Chelsea ignored the deputy.

"I'm leaving early," she said slowly, as if she was talking to a two-year-old. "I have a date and I need to get ready."

"A date?" Carter ambled over as if he hadn't a care in the world, but Jess recognized the signs of a jealous male. Poor Carter. The kid didn't know he was dealing with one of the smartest young women in the county. "Who with?"

"It's really none of your business," she said, and turned sideways so Carter could get a good look at her legs, then hopped off the desk. "I'm leaving early," she repeated, "if you don't mind, boss."

"Go."

Carter wouldn't stop. "It's not like I won't know," he said. "I'll see you around town tonight. I'm working, you know."

"I know," she said. "If I see you I'll wave." She picked up her purse and was out the door in three seconds flat.

"What's up with her?"

Jess shrugged. "She's got a date."

"She's usually nicer to me."

"You usually ignore her," Jess pointed out, then wondered why the hell he was giving advice. He leaned forward, restacked his files and looked at the clock. "I'm going home early, too, Carter. The place is yours."

"Really?"

"Yeah. I hope it's as quiet as last Friday night was. If not, you know how to reach me."

He was going home. To move furniture, build shelves, give the future dining room a second coat of white paint...and to stay as far away physically from his wife as possible.

"I'M CONCERNED about your blood pressure," Dr. Bradford said, setting aside Lorna's chart. "It's still too high. We're going to do a few tests to see what's going on. I don't think it's a case of preeclampsia, but I want to make sure."

"And preeclampsia is—?" Lorna prompted. She gave Jess her hand and he helped her sit up on the examining table. She didn't let his hand go.

"A condition of pregnancy that produces high blood pressure, swelling in the face and hands, excessive protein in the urine. It can be dangerous if not treated properly, but it goes away once the baby is born. Let's not worry about it until we know whether you have it." She smiled reassuringly, but Jess didn't feel at all reassured. His wife looked as calm as if she'd been told something about the weather.

"What do I do about it?"

"Are you still working at the café?"

"No. I haven't been for a couple of weeks, since we got married."

"Good. And congratulations on your marriage, by the way." The doctor turned to Jess. "Your wife is going to need plenty of rest. Can you see that she gets it?"

"Of course," he replied. "Is there something dangerous going on here?"

"We'll know after we run some more tests," she replied. "It may be as simple as pregnancy-induced hypertension, but we're not going to take any chances." She looked at the chart again, then to Lorna. "You have nine weeks left, Mrs. Sheridan. And we're going to make sure you have a healthy baby. I'll send the nurse in with instructions for the next few weeks plus the paperwork for the lab tests."

"Thank you," she said, but Jess didn't say a word. She attempted to release his hand, but he wouldn't let go. "Jess?"

"What?"

"You can let go now."

"Oh." He looked down at their joined hands and loosened his fingers. Then he turned to face her. "Are you okay?"

"Scared to death," she admitted. "But down deep I think everything's going to be okay."

"How?"

She shrugged. "I don't know. I just feel it."

"It's my fault."

"Why do you think that?"

"I should never have had...have done...well, you know. The wedding night."

"I don't think sex and high blood pressure are connected."

"I hope you're right," he managed to respond. He wanted to wrap his arms around Lorna and not let go until he was sure she and the baby were safe, but he felt helpless. It almost seemed as if his heart had turned stone cold with fear. What the hell was going on?

He'd never thought that anything could go wrong. But then, that's what he'd thought when he was married to Susan, too.

FOR LORNA, this seemed like the slowest nine days of her life. Elizabeth and Emily visited, passing the time with talk of decorating nurseries and what to name the babies. Her father drove down four times and brought frozen chicken pot pies, fresh fruit salads and various bags of cookies.

And Jess went to work and came home again, polite and kind and distant. He was a man doing his duty, Lorna realized, and he intended to do it well. But showing affection was out of the question.

Expecting affection was only setting herself up for disappointment. And here she'd thought—foolishly, she knew now—that somehow everything would work out just fine. Their forced marriage would become one of love, she and the baby would defy high blood pressure and be fine, and the world would spin happily along without problems to solve or pain to endure.

She was wrong. Her hormones must have made her delusional. Her husband didn't love her and didn't show signs that he ever would, except for those two times in bed.

Even that advantage was gone. Lovemaking was impossible now. *Unthinkable* now. She wondered if she would ever want to make love to Jess again. Emily had assured her that she was only going through a phase and after she'd given birth and the baby started sleeping through the night, then the man in the bed beside her would start looking pretty good again.

If there was still a man beside her in the bed when this was all over with.

So Lorna lay on the couch and read magazines. She slept. Emily taught her how to crochet and Elizabeth brought her a needlepoint kit, with pastel alphabet letters, to make a picture for the nursery. The Bennett children brought cookies and let her read stories to them. She wrote thank-you notes for the amazing array of wedding presents, she sent Chelsea flowers for organizing the reception, and she worried about using disposable diapers or fabric ones. She took her blood pressure daily, having been loaned a machine by the doctor. She rested on her side, as advised. She went into the office once a week for tests and she counted the days until this would be over.

Meanwhile Jess went to work each morning, unless he was on the evening shift. He bought groceries, he made dinners and he helped her in and out of chairs.

All in the line of duty.

"WE NEED A NAME."

"For what?"

There was no answer to his question, so after a long moment of silence Jess looked over to the couch where Lorna was resting for the evening. She had a stack of books beside her and a notebook in her hand.

"For the baby." The look she gave him made it clear she thought he was an idiot.

"Oh." He put down his pen and set his paperwork aside. Criminal statistics and triplicate reports could wait. He hated it when Lorna looked at him like that. Come to think of it, she'd looked at him like that a lot today. "Shoot."

"Do you have any preferences?"

"As long as it's not Jester, Junior."

"Family names? Friends? Your father?"

"My father is Jim. My grandfather was Jester. His father was a James. We don't need to keep that going," he said.

"Why is your sister named Ricky?"

"It's really Rebecca, but she thought that sounded too tame for a rock and blues singer."

"Rebecca's a nice name for a girl," Lorna mused, scribbling something on the pad.

"For someone else's girl."

"Oh." She frowned at her list. "I'm having trouble with girls' names. What do you think of Sarah, Leah, Beth, Heather or Jane?"

He stared at her. "I can't picture a girl. And I can't picture a girl with any of those names."

"Then picture a boy." Now she was starting to sound exasperated.

His pager went off, which, come to think of it, was pretty good timing. "I have to go."

He paused on his way out the front door, but he couldn't think of anything to say. Lorna looked beautiful and tired and very, very sad. "I'm sorry, Lorna. About the names. About having to leave. About everything."

"It's okay," she said, looking up at him with blue eyes that held tears. "Really, it is. Don't worry about the names. I'll come up with something acceptable."

Jess wanted to go to her, but he stood there as if he was nailed down to the wood floor.

"We'll talk about it in the morning," he promised, and hoped that would be true. What could he say to make anything better between them? They were two strangers living together who had no choice but to make the best of things.

"Jess?"

He paused with his hand on the doorknob. "What?"

"Happy Valentine's Day." Her voice was soft, her expression almost wistful. In other words, he was in deep shit.

Thirty minutes later and in a bar ten miles north of town, Bobby Calhoun agreed with him.

"You forgot it was Valentine's Day? I thought you married guys were smarter than that," he said, finishing his beer.

"You thought wrong."

"You could probably get some flowers at the grocery store," the young man said. "You want a beer?"

"Can't. I'm on duty. Carter needed help breaking up a fight out front. I just came inside to make sure it was quiet."

"It's a busy night," the young cowboy said, looking around at the couples cozied up to the bar. "I've got a dinner date myself."

"Guess I'd better go buy flowers."

"Don't forget the card."

"Right." He started to leave, but Bobby hollered to him.

"Hey, Sheridan?"

"Yeah?" He hoped the grocery store would be open for a while longer. Maybe they would have roses again. Yellow ones to match her hair.

"Did you get my message?"

"No." Or daisies. Lorna seemed like the daisy type. She might not think he was an idiot if he brought daisies and one of those cards with lots of glitter.

"The lawyer has the papers for the ranch. Look 'em over and let me know what you want to do."

"Yeah, thanks. I'll do that first thing tomorrow."

Bobby waved, and Jess hurried out of the bar. He wondered why his deputy was still hanging around the parking lot, but he didn't stop to ask. There wasn't time.

He was almost back in Beauville when the accident happened.

LORNA WAS JUST ABOUT FINISHED with the new list of names when her water broke. Suddenly the backache she'd experienced all day seemed more intense and the pressure in her lower abdomen increased. She managed to get off the couch and retrieve the phone, but suddenly nothing was easy. She called her doctor, whose assistant suggested she come to the hospital in Marysville to be examined.

She called Jess on his pager number, but it was Carter who called her back soon after she called Emily. And it was Carter who brought Chelsea to the house at the same time that Emily hurried across the street. Bobby Calhoun walked in right behind them.

"Where's Jess?" she asked everyone standing in her living room.

"He's, uh, still at another emergency," Chelsea said. Her earrings, rows of glittery red hearts, dangled to her bare shoulders and matched the short red dress that barely covered her thighs. Lorna spared one sigh of envy for Chelsea's waist before another contraction hit her.

"Can you tell him I have to go to the hospital now?"

"Sure," Chelsea said. "I'll get word."

Bobby stepped forward. "Want me to drive you? I've got the Caddy and it goes real fast when it has to."

"Maybe we should call the ambulance." Emily put her arm around Lorna's shoulder and eased her into a chair. "Just in case. This baby is eight weeks early."

Carter shook his head. "Can't," he said. "It's bein' used."

Lorna sucked in her breath and waited for the contraction to pass. "There's only one ambulance?"

"It's a small town," Carter said, as if that explained everything. Chelsea glared at him.

"Carter," she snapped. "We'll take your car. You can turn the lights and the siren on and we'll get there in no time at all."

"We?" he asked.

"What about dinner?" Bobby's face fell. "I got roses in the car for you."

Chelsea ignored both of them and turned to Lorna instead. "I have some paramedic training from when I was in the volunteer fire department. I guess that'll have to do."

"I guess," Lorna agreed. According to all the books she'd read, these contractions weren't supposed to come this fast. But then, according to the books, the baby wasn't supposed to come this early, either.

Emily didn't look at all convinced. "Have you ever delivered a baby, Chelsea?"

"Just once. After a fire."

"That's good enough for me," Lorna said. "Help me get to the police car, will you?"

"I'm going, too," Emily declared. "Bobby, go across the street to my house and tell George what's going on. And then go find the sheriff."

"Yes, ma'am," the cowboy said, helping Lorna to her feet. "I'm real sorry about your Valentine's Day, ma'am. I know the sheriff went off to buy you some flowers, so don't be too mad at him."

"I'm not mad at him," Lorna said. "Just because he forgot about Valentine's Day and isn't here to take me to the hospital to have his baby, doesn't mean I'm mad."

"Yes, ma'am," Bobby said, but he backed up a step. "You sound real happy to me."

12

"Is my husband here yet?"

"Not yet, Mrs. Sheridan," the nurse said. She checked the various monitors and machines that Lorna was hooked up to. "But this seems to be a big night for having babies. We've got husbands all over the place."

"But not mine." Lorna was beginning to feel very, very sorry for herself.

"Don't worry. He'll show up sooner or later."

"He's a sheriff," Lorna insisted. "He has a car with lights on top. He went to buy flowers. How hard can it be to find him?"

"I'm sure he'll walk in the door any minute."

Lorna wasn't so sure, despite the nurse's soothing tone. How could Jess disappear like this?

"Knock, knock," Emily said from the doorway to Lorna's room. "Feel like company?"

"In between contractions," she said. "They're coming faster."

"What did the doctor say?"

"The baby can survive being eight weeks early, but

will be monitored for lung problems and anything else." Another contraction began again, so Lorna panted and breathed and counted the way the book had instructed until it subsided.

Meanwhile Emily made herself comfortable in a bedside chair and held Lorna's hand. "All set?"

"Yes." She leaned back against the pillows. "I wish I'd had time to attend the birthing classes at the library. Has anyone seen Jess?"

"Chelsea's working on it. She has a cell phone, a pager and some kind of little computer. Do you think she carries all that stuff around in her purse?"

"She has the confidence of ten women. Did you see that dress?"

"Half the doctors in the hospital have passed by the waiting area to look. She's caused quite a commotion all over the hospital."

"Those were the days." The women shared a smile, but then Lorna's expression changed. "He might not come tonight. He had to marry me, Em. He never wanted the baby and he never wanted me."

"He'll be here," her friend promised. "I know he will."

"Maybe. He'll do his duty." Lorna braced herself for another contraction. "But right now I don't think that's going to be enough for me."

CHELSEA KNEW if she were left alone to run the world—or at least her small part of it—things would go a lot smoother. Off-duty sheriffs would not land in the middle of car accidents, pregnant women would give birth exactly when scheduled and deputy sheriffs would be less handsome and a heck of a lot smarter.

"I said," she repeated to Carter via cell phone, "find out if the sheriff was *in* the accident." She couldn't hear his reply and since using cell phones wasn't allowed in the hospital, she clicked the off button, then folded the phone and tucked it in her purse.

"Answer the page, boss," she muttered, afraid to think of the one reason he wouldn't call her back. She'd heard from Jess, a garbled message about an accident. She'd notified the ambulance and given them what little information she had. Immediately afterward Lorna had called to tell her husband she was in labor. Bobby had arrived to pick her up and found her talking into two phones. Carter, finally acting jealous, had followed Bobby to her house.

Both men had eyed that red dress for a nice long time, Chelsea remembered. Carter had looked like he wanted to cry. "We won't tell Lorna about the accident," Chelsea made them promise. "Not until we know the boss is okay."

Now they really had lost him. She'd checked with the emergency room twice, but there was no sheriff. And everyone was too busy to tell her anything, except for one young resident who wished her a Happy Valentine's Day and asked her if she was free at midnight to have a drink.

She told him she'd keep that offer in mind. After tonight's events, alcohol might be especially welcome.

Chelsea pulled out her phone again and, ignoring all hospital rules, dialed Jess's pager again. "Answer, damn it," she whispered. "Your wife needs you."

JESS NEEDED MORE than a Valentine's card and a bunch of flowers wrapped in colored tissue, but he hoped for the best when he arrived home to deliver them to his wife. He would have to tell her about the accident, about Mike Monterro's fatal heart attack while driving home from town. There would be tears, but he would comfort her. He intended to be better at that sort of thing from now on.

When he walked through the door, every light was on in the house, but there was no Lorna. Where would a pregnant woman go at nine o'clock on a weeknight? Was she so disgusted with him she'd left him?

It was possible, he realized, calling her name as he walked through the small house. In his short time at the job, he hadn't been the greatest husband.

And according to his ex-wife, he'd never been good at that job to begin with, but would Lorna leave him over a less-than-romantic Valentine's Day? There was no note. If she was having the baby she would have contacted him.

When the phone rang, Jess lunged for it. George Bennett's calm voice explained everything, but Jess only heard the first sentence: Lorna was in the hospital having the baby.

He turned on the siren and the lights and drove faster than he ever had in the call of duty. The same thoughts went over and over in his head: the baby was going to be born too early, Lorna had high blood pressure, the labor had been sudden and, worst of all, Carter and Chelsea were in charge.

All of this could have been avoided if he hadn't lost his pager. At least he'd remembered to grab the flowers and the card on his way out the door.

SOME SADIST TOLD HER to push, and to keep pushing. Lorna concentrated on pushing and panting and following directions while Emily stood next to her and quietly cheered her on.

"This pushing thing actually works?" Lorna asked.

"Yes, Mrs. Sheridan," a nurse assured her. "This is the way it's done most of the time. Just hang in there a few minutes more."

"Good news," Emily said. "Your husband just walked through the door."

Lorna blinked and, sure enough, Jess was heading toward her. He wore blue scrubs like the nurses and

Emily, but his face was pale. "You're not going to faint again, are you?"

He swallowed and avoided looking anywhere but into her eyes as he hurried toward her. "No. Except maybe with relief." Emily stepped back and Jess brushed his fingers across Lorna's damp cheek. "Are you okay?"

"Where have you been?"

"There was an accident outside of town. I lost my pager. Are you really okay?"

"Push," the doctor said. "And keep pushing until I tell you to stop."

She pushed, but managed to grit her teeth and spit out, "Do-I-*look*-okay?"

"They get cranky at this stage, Mr. Sheridan," a nurse explained. "Oh, boy, here's the head."

"Stop pushing," someone said.

"What are they doing?"

"Cleaning its face," Jess said. "It's okay."

Nothing was okay. She was being split in two after being driven to Marysville by a suicidal deputy. "Where the hell have you been?"

"Push again, Mrs. Sheridan, and we'll have a baby here!"

She pushed for what seemed like a century. She braced herself, clung to Jess's hand, and pushed until she heard Dr. Bradford announce, "It's a boy."

"A boy," her husband breathed.

"A boy?" She didn't have a name for a boy. "Really?"

"He's got all the right equipment," a nurse said, right before the baby started screaming.

"Can I see him?"

"In two seconds," the doctor promised. "Somebody help the father out of here," she said. "He's the delicate type."

Lorna didn't want to laugh, but she couldn't help it. She felt as if she'd run a marathon and won first place. Her son was placed on her chest. He was tiny and red, screaming and waving his little fingers, but he was the most beautiful baby she had ever seen. She choked back tears as she tried to comfort him. "Is he going to be all right?"

"He's looking good," the pediatrician said. He picked him up and tucked him into a waiting blanket. "We're going to check him out now and I'll be in to see you later."

Emily patted Lorna's shoulder. "He's beautiful."

"He is, isn't he?"

"Absolutely."

Later, when she'd been settled in her room in the maternity ward, Lorna waited for her husband. And waited for her son. And, before she dozed off, wondered how on earth she'd ever thought they could become a family.

JESS WALKED A FEW LAPS around the hospital parking lot and inhaled lots of fresh air before venturing inside. The nurses had fussed over him, given him an ice pack and made him breathe into a paper bag for a few minutes. Then he'd rushed to the nursery, only to discover that the doctor was still examining the baby.

He stopped when he got out of the elevator. He needed to find Lorna. And he thought about calling his parents, who were still in the Grand Canyon as far as anyone knew. He should call Ricky. And he had to find Chelsea. The last time he'd seen her she'd been giving her phone number to a muscular paramedic while Carter looked suicidal.

The elevator doors pinged to announce more arrivals, so Jess moved out of the way as a stocky bald man shoved his way past a couple of nurses' aides.

"Texas Tom?" Jess drew himself up to his full height.

"Yeah?" Clearly he didn't recognize the man he'd hit with barbecue tongs last July.

"What are you doing on the maternity ward?"

Tom's chest puffed up with pride. "What the hell do you think I'm doing? I'm here to see my son."

"Like hell you are," Jess muttered, right before he took a swing at the BBQ King's ruddy oversize nose. "That kid is *mine.*"

The crunch of bone under his fist was extremely satisfying.

"SHOULD I ARREST HIM?" Carter turned to Chelsea and grabbed his handcuffs.

"Which one would you arrest?" she asked. "The innocent bystander barbecue creep or your boss?"

"Well, since you put it that way," he said, and tucked the handcuffs into his belt again.

"No one's arresting anyone," Jess declared, flexing his fist. He'd forgotten how much a good punch like that could hurt. "We're just settling an old score."

"We are?" Tom asked, seated on the floor with an ice pack on his nose.

"You hit me from behind last summer. I owed you." And there was no way in hell that Lorna had just had Texas Tom's baby. So what if the baby was eight weeks early. So what if Tom was there to see it. Circumstantial evidence didn't mean a whole lot.

"He's insane," Tom grumbled. "I never hit no one."

"And stay away from my wife," Jess warned. "And my son."

A nurse replaced Tom's ice pack with a bandage for his nose. "No one be-lieveth me," he complained. "Inthane. He'th inthane."

Jess ignored him and felt queasy again. He'd just realized he was in love with his wife and he damn well didn't want to find out that she'd married him under false pretenses. "Where is she?"

"Room 214," Chelsea said. "Don't wake her up."

He was pretty good at waking her up, Jess thought. That's how they made a baby. But he tiptoed into the double room, empty on the left side, and watched his sleeping wife until she woke up and smiled at him.

"I love you," he said, which made her stare at him with those wide blue eyes. "And if that boy is Texas Tom's, I don't care. We're married and we're going to stay that way." He set the drooping roses on the nightstand, but somewhere along the way he'd lost the card. "Happy Valentine's Day."

"Jess," she said carefully, as if she was coming out of a fog. "What does Texas Tom have to do with anything?"

"I don't know and I don't care. I don't *want* to know." He grinned. "I think I broke his nose. Don't worry, he won't be bothering you."

"You think the baby is Texas Tom's?"

"I don't care if he is or not," Jess insisted. "Though all of the evidence—never mind," he said, noticing her frown. "We'll never speak of it again. I do love you. More than I ever thought I could love anyone. And I have your Valentine's card in the car."

"I think you'd better leave," was all his wife said. "Before I take your gun and shoot you."

"Huh?"

"There are bullets in that thing, right?"

Jess backed up and left the room. He'd read about postpartum depression and it didn't sound like a

hell of a lot of fun. Good thing there was medication
for it. He'd have to ask the nurse to get some.

"HE LOOKS JUST LIKE Grandpa," Ricky said. "All
skinny and bony, with that forehead and those
knobby knees."

The infant was the spitting image of James Sheridan, rancher and truck driver, terrific storyteller and
lousy fiddler. Obviously there was no barbecue sauce
in his genes, unless Lorna had cooks in her family.

"What a relief," Lorna muttered, holding her baby
with gentle hands.

"Yes," Ricky said, misunderstanding. "He's doing
really well for a preemie, isn't he?"

"I don't get to have him much," Lorna said.
"They're keeping an eye on him, but his lungs seem
okay. As soon as he gains some weight they might
even let him come home."

"Your in-laws will be descending upon you real
soon," Ricky promised. "They'll probably camp in
the parking lot until the baby goes home."

"My father can't stay away either," Lorna said. "I
sent him home this afternoon to rest."

"Speaking of rest, I should let you get some." Ricky
stood and took another peek at her nephew. "He's
darling. I wonder if he'll be musical. With those long
fingers he might be a pretty good guitarist."

Lorna smiled down at her son and Jess thought his

heart would explode. He'd never in his wildest dreams thought that such a thing was possible. The only problem seemed to be that Lorna wasn't talking to him, so Jess said goodbye to his sister and shut the door behind her. There wasn't much privacy in the hospital, but he'd have to do his best.

"So," he began, watching Lorna rearrange the baby's blankets, "I guess I made a fool of myself."

"Yes." She didn't look at him.

"Not the first time."

"No." She sighed and looked up at him. "You hit Texas Tom."

"Yeah." There was no sense denying something that everyone in the hospital was talking about.

"Good," Lorna said, flashing a brief smile. "He deserved it. But his wife is going to wonder how he broke his nose while she was having a baby."

"Am I forgiven?" He stepped closer to the bed, within touching distance of his wife and his son.

"Only if you meant what you said last night." She gave him that come-to-bed smile that never failed to cause his body to react. He should have been ashamed of himself, but he figured he'd be like this until he was ninety, as long as Lorna was around to smile at him.

"The 'I love you' part?"

"The 'more than I thought I could ever love anyone' part."

"Absolutely." He sat on the edge of the bed and kissed his beautiful wife's mouth. "More than I've ever loved anyone."

"Wait a minute," she said, once she caught her breath. "Are you buying your old ranch back because you wish you still lived there with your first wife?"

It took a second for that to sink in. "I'm not buying it at all," he said. "I think we have everything we need right now." He looked down at his sleeping son and knew he would give his life to protect him, then faced his wife. "Don't you?"

"I love you," she whispered. "I always have."

"Honey," Jess said, cradling both of them in his arms, "do you think they'd let all three of us take a nap in this bed?"

"No. They're going to kick you out." She leaned against him. "But in about six weeks, I'm going to wake you up and make you show me how much you love me."

"Yes, ma'am," the sheriff said to his wife. "And I'll be right there ready and waiting for you."

_____Epilogue_____

SIX WEEKS TO THE DAY after his son's birth, Jess Sheridan made love to his wife. His son, Benjamin Michael, slept soundly in the other room and nicely gave his parents several hours of peace and quiet.

"Now," Jess said, rousing his sleepy wife. She smiled but didn't open her eyes. "I've waited long enough."

"For what?" She snuggled deeper under the covers, her naked body touching his in a most satisfactory way. "You just _got_ what you've been waiting for, didn't you?"

"For these," he said, and leaned over the bed to find the bag he'd left nearby. Jess dropped the velvet pouch near Lorna's nose. "A gift of love. Isn't that what you said?"

She looked at him, then at the bag. And then she sat up, revealing a body he'd never tire of admiring. "Jess?"

"Will you wear them now?" He watched as she turned the bag upside down and let the three rings fall into the palm of her hand. And then he watched her start to cry. "Oh, no. Not the hormones again."

"No," she sniffed. "I was thinking of Mike. And how much he loved his wife. I can't believe he left us his house."

His house...and one of the sweetest ranches in the county, Jess wanted to add. He was still reeling over the reading of the will. Turned out that old man had no family and a sentimental streak a mile wide.

"I didn't mean to make you sad. You don't have to take the rings if you don't want them," he said, trying to hide his disappointment. "I thought since I screwed up Valentine's Day, I'd try to make up for it."

"You did, you idiot," his loving wife replied. "You gave me the sweetest baby in Beauville."

"He also has your temper," Jess pointed out. "Do you want the rings or not?"

"Of course I do. And I hope Ben didn't inherit your way with words." She leaned over and kissed him. "I love the rings. Thank you." She inched closer. "Want to let me go to sleep so you can wake me up and make love to me all over again?"

"The last time that happened we made a baby," he warned, settling himself under the covers so that his body stretched against her.

"And look how perfect it turned out," Lorna said, closing her eyes. Within seconds she was asleep, so Jess picked up the rings that had fallen onto the quilt and tucked them into their pouch for safekeeping.

"I love you," he whispered, trying not to wake her up, but Lorna snuggled closer and mumbled something he couldn't understand.

"What?" he said, not sure if she was awake or not.

"Stay," she said, her hand on his chest. As if she thought he was going to leave her?

Jess wanted to laugh, but instead he covered his wife's hand with his own and, even doubting she could hear him, solemnly promised, "Honey, I'm not going anywhere."

Jess Sheridan might have had no use for weddings, but he was a man in love with his wife.

Come back to Beauville, Texas
next month
for
Kristine Rolofson's

BLAME IT ON TEXAS

The BOOTS & BEAUTIES *miniseries continues*
in Kristine's first Harlequin single title.
Available at all bookstores March 2001.

Pamela Burford presents

The Wedding Ring

*Four high school friends and a pact—
every girl gets her ideal mate by thirty or be
prepared for matchmaking! The rules are
simple. Give your "chosen" man three
months...and see what happens!*

Love's Funny That Way
Temptation #812—on sale December 2000
It's no joke when Raven Muldoon falls in love with comedy
club owner Hunter—*brother* of her "intended."

I Do, But Here's the Catch
Temptation #816—on sale January 2001
Charli Ross is more than willing to give up her status as
last of a dying breed—the thirty-year-old virgin—to Grant.
But all *he* wants is marriage.

One Eager Bride To Go
Temptation #820—on sale February 2001
Sunny Bleecker is still waiting tables at Wafflemania when
Kirk comes home from California and wants to marry her.
It's as if all her dreams have finally come true—except...

Fiancé for Hire
Temptation #824—on sale March 2001
No way is Amanda Coppersmith going to let
The Wedding Ring rope her into marriage. But no matter
how clever she is, Nick is one step ahead of her...

**"Pamela Burford creates the
memorable characters readers love!"
—*The Literary Times***

#1 *New York Times* bestselling author

NORA ROBERTS

brings you more of the loyal and loving,
tempestuous and tantalizing Stanislaski family.

Coming in February 2001

The Stanislaski Sisters

Natasha and Rachel

Though raised in the Old World traditions of their
family, fiery Natasha Stanislaski and cool, classy
Rachel Stanislaski are ready for a *new* world of love....

*And also available in February 2001 from
Silhouette Special Edition, the newest book in the
heartwarming Stanislaski saga*

CONSIDERING KATE

Natasha and Spencer Kimball's daughter Kate turns her
back on old dreams and returns to her hometown, where
she finds the *man* of her dreams.

Available at your favorite retail outlet.

Where love comes alive™

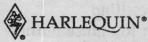

HARLEQUIN®

makes any time special—online...

eHARLEQUIN.com

your romantic escapes

—Indulgences—

♥ Monthly guides to indulging yourself,
such as:
  ★ **Tub Time:** A guide for bathing beauties
  ★ **Magic Massages:** A treat for tired feet

—Horoscopes—

♥ Find your daily Passionscope, weekly
Lovescopes and Erotiscopes

♥ Try our compatibility game

—Reel Love—

♥ Read all the latest romantic
movie reviews

—Royal Romance—

♥ Get the latest scoop on your favorite
royal romances

—Romantic Travel—

♥ For the most romantic destinations, hotels
and travel activities

HINTE1

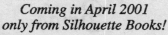

HARLEQUIN®

bestselling authors

Merline Lovelace
Deborah Simmons
Julia Justiss

cordially invite you to enjoy three
brand-new stories of unexpected love

The Officer's Bride

Available April 2001

HARLEQUIN®
Makes any time special®

Visit us at www.eHarlequin.com   PHOFFICER